Elsewhere

Cover design by Donald E. Munson.

Book design by Iris Bass.

Elsewhere

JONATHAN STRONG

AVAILABLE
PRESS

BALLANTINE BOOKS • NEW YORK

An Available Press Book

Copyright © 1985 by Jonathan Strong
The first section of ELSEWHERE originally appeared in SHENANDOAH.

All rights reserved under International and Pan-American Copyright Conventions.
Published in the United States by Ballantine Books, a division of Random
House, Inc., New York, and simultaneously in Canada by Random House of
Canada Limited, Toronto.

Library of Congress Catalog Card Number: 84-91744

ISBN 0-345-31911-7

Manufactured in the United States of America

First Edition: March 1985

for Morgan

Soliloquy

Our baby has been taken—not actually my baby, but her baby, and his. He fathered her, I gave her and her mother a home. We have an idea where she is, we know who took her, when and why, but we don't think we will get her back. He didn't know what he was leaving us with when he died.

His sister is at the heart of it, but she didn't dare take the baby herself. Now she's making money off the book she has called The Letters of My Dead Brother. It didn't take much for her to put it together, just her own memories, which someone else must have written down for her because her own writing is terrible, and then all his letters, his words. If I had lived elsewhere I would have letters too, but I lived here, near him, and so did Nell, my wife.

I had all of them in high school, him and his sister, and the baby thief, and Nell too. I remember what hopeless compositions his sister wrote and how surprised I was when he came along seven years later and wrote the way he did. He started his Soliloquy when he was in my class, and after he had me, he kept writing. If he hadn't done so much of his own already at eighteen, she wouldn't be able to make money on him now. Her dead brother, possibly a suicide, is one thing; her dead brother who was so promising, whom you might even have heard of, or read something by, is another. Her book is now in bookstores in the city. I bought a copy so I could read more words written by him, even if they were written to her. But with the money she makes she will protect herself further, and our baby will never come back to us.

Nell is only a girl. She is out of her mind not knowing what to do. She lost him first, and then her family told her to get out, and now her baby has been taken. I'm not able to do enough to help. She stays at my house, at our house, trembling, and when I come home from work I hold her and bring her supper and sit with her. When we go out, she looks like anyone else on the street, but she won't call up her old friends. She might as well come from out of town. Together we look in stores, at nothing of interest. She has no interest left. We make our rounds and come home.

She isn't any less the skinny Nell Parshall from the class below his. She has her freckly skin and long dry fluffy hair and the little twisting of her neck when she talks. I don't know how she'd feel to read the book of letters. I keep my copy here at my new job. She would want to read more words written by him, but I'm afraid to show her. There are things he says in there about her that would jolt her. If I stick by her, slowly and carefully, will she come back up to herself, stop trembling? Should I take her to a doctor, some sort of counselor, a priest even? I've told her we can eventually get divorced, and she can start again if she wants to, but she doesn't have to if she doesn't want to because I will stay with her the rest of my life. She has to know I will, not be afraid I won't. What else can I do?

For me it is the outcome of when he first stayed after class. "Mr. Stokes," he said, "I have some writing I've done extra."

He hadn't shown me a thing for class, or said anything yet, but I had taken note of his uncommon last name on the class list and had to ask if he had a sister named Elsa. He nodded. "I had her the first year I taught here," I said. "How is she? Where did she go?"

"She moved out west. She's married," he said. "I haven't seen her for a year, but I write her."

I asked him what was the extra writing he'd been doing.

"Just some short things," he said, "if you want to see them. I haven't shown them to anyone."

Then I remembered a long-winded composition his sister had written about a little brother who had taken the stuffed cat she kept on her pillow and hidden it, and she caught him talking cat talk to it in the crawlspace under the stairs.

"I remember doing that," he said with a happy smile I hadn't yet seen on his face. "I forgot I'd done that."

He was a dark-eyed boy of fifteen. I had certainly noticed him in the first weeks on the far side of the room. Close up, he had especially smooth skin tight across evident bones, his cheeks, his chin, his wrists, nothing satisfied-looking about him. But he didn't look in flux, or on the verge, like a teenager. He looked as if he'd always looked like that and always would.

"I don't want to bother you with it," he said, eyes downcast. "I don't mean it for extra credit." Then when he handed me his notebook, his eyes flashed from timidity to what I saw as ardor.

I didn't have time to look at the notebook till the weekend. When I did look I sensed at once how important to me he would become, a boy who could write like that and seemed so alone. In everything he described there was always a lonely watcher, the soliloquist, I supposed. Could I become important to him? What I wrote carefully in the margins with my extra-fine ballpoint was a wispy commentary on his thick blue still wet-looking strokes.

When I handed him his notebook after class, I said, "Come talk to me about my comments," but he didn't. A month later he let me take the notebook again.

"Do you mind if I don't talk about it for a while?" he asked. "If I just write it?"

I sat at my desk trying to be a little indifferent. "Whatever is most helpful to you," I said. "But you have to keep up your class work too. Can't you copy something from the notebook for class?"

"I don't mean it to count," he said.

"Then you'll have to do something else for class," I said. Soon he began to catch up on the exercises and reports he'd gotten behind in.

His school record gave his address as the Saint Vincent Home, and he did look like he should be an orphan. He had only a few changes of clothes. The thick black sweater he wore when it got colder brought his sister back to my eyes. She had been as dark, and she always seemed engulfed in a black sweater.

His writing told me nothing about his life. He didn't write homey anecdotes the way his sister had. I asked Paula Innocenzo, when we were having our coffee in the faculty room, what she remembered of Elsa. She slouched back on the fat vinyl cushion, air hissing out its vents, and stared into her coffee as if reading a fortune. "Dark and shy, very earnest, her parents expected a lot, I remember. That father! I can still see the flourishes of his signature on the long angry notes I'd get from him."

"You have your share of parent trouble," I said. She had been embroiled with Liam McGee's family all that week.

"But Elsa's father was immeasurably worse," she said. "He'd come in and badger me, really badger me. He'd tell me his life story, how he'd made his way in this country. I was too stupid to recognize his daughter's promise, her talents. He could tell, even if he didn't speak English too well. And who was I to be an English teacher anyway! There was none of that smiley innuendo I get from the McGees. But didn't her father ever come yell at you?"

I couldn't remember him. I just remembered the girl in the big sweater lingering by my desk to talk about her compositions. I probably gave her better grades than Paula did. Elsa did put in more effort than most.

"You'll be getting her little brother next year," I said. "He seems to live in a church home, Saint Vincent's. I suppose that means their parents are dead."

Paula looked up at me. "Do you suppose? Well, that's a sad thought," she said. "I wouldn't have missed him, but you expect to keep crossing paths with a character like that, and to think you won't ever—" She looked down, resting her lips on the rim of her cup. "He was there at her graduation, beaming away. That's the last I saw of him. Elsa wasn't one of my devoted followers."

"There was a period when she tried to be mine," I said, remembering.

"The Saint Vincent Home is down the hill," said Paula, "down the back side, I mean, a rundown sort of place. What some of these kids are faced with! Orphanages, the McGees for parents—"

My faster track of tenth graders usually went on to Paula for eleventh. I was lucky to have had Liam McGee when he was still doing his work. He even developed a casual sort of attachment to me. He'd drop by my apartment after school, in the evenings too when he should have been at home. That next year with Paula he was in need of something more, and he kept dropping by, too often for me to feel entirely comfortable about it. I began to act a bit less welcoming.

Once when he passed me in the hall at a change of classes, he said, loud enough to attract a few heads, "Hey, you've got Ogna Santy this year! He told me you were his best teacher."

Careful to take all praise in stride, never to show delight, I said, "Is that so?"

"He's a good kid," said Liam, quickly lost in the hall crowd.

When Liam next dropped by my apartment, I asked how long they'd known each other.

"I'd better not say more about him," he said, "because what he likes about talking to you, Mr. Stokes, is that you don't know anything about him. That's what he told me. I don't want to spoil it."

"That's an odd reason of his," I said.

Liam said, "It's for his writing. He's real serious, not an asshole like me. I don't know, I never saw his writing. He wants someone who doesn't like him or he doesn't know to help him with it."

Liam had a sensible side. He didn't like to show it, but I used to think it could rescue him from the worst, and maybe it still will.

What can I do to rescue Nell? She hasn't seen her old friends for months, though they must want to see her. Her parents haven't called, but her aunt called me at work once to find out how she was, probably to pass on news. Sometimes thinking about my in-laws, I imagine that this has all come about a different way, that I have ended up with Nell because I fell in love with her, that our families have met and made friends. But it doesn't hold, because the Parshalls are only a couple of years older than I, really, and my parents are old and don't travel. Nell's aunt was cold and matter-of-fact with me. Why did I want her to say a kind thing, even to thank me?

I find myself missing the baby. Why shouldn't I? Though I only knew her for a few weeks, she seemed like mine. We named her Antonia after her father. At first she had lots of dark hair, just beginning to fall out when she was taken. Nell walks around the house with nothing to hold. She goes up the staircase, circling around, to the top under the skylight, stands and looks down, then comes slowly down again, holding herself at the waist. It is a bad house for her to live in. I've thought she might jump from the top landing, but she promises she won't. In any house, wouldn't she find some way if she wanted to?

I don't think she wants to. Nell used to be sure of her feelings, not shaky. She was good for him, as I was, and he was lucky to have us. His sister wouldn't help him. And Liam really couldn't, or his friend Ladro. But we could, we did. It was only at the last we didn't help him enough. How could she not have gone on to have the baby after that?

I have felt like a father. I have gotten up with her when she cried, bought the big boxes of diapers at the supermarket, and the people in line must have thought I was a father. I loved to change Antonia's diapers, to wipe her off and have her smile at me. It's not long since we had her. I bought a camera and took a roll of pictures. I can see her face in every light. I can see Nell on the stairs with her, Nell in her plaid robe, the baby a white package in her arms.

Antonia had her own room between ours. I moved my study to the unfinished top floor, but the weather was warm enough already. I untaped the plastic sheets on the windows, and there was our view, down the hill over the rooftops of our town to the city skyline. Nell would bring her up to sit in the sun, her white blanket on the rough boards. "This will be a bad house when she starts to crawl," I said. "We'll put up gates everywhere."

"When will she crawl, Burt?" Nell asked me, looking up from beside her baby.

I was at my desk, almost as though I was still at school, having a conference with Nell Parshall after class, two years back. "Maybe at nine months," I said. I wasn't sure. "Some babies don't crawl. They go straight to walking. They tell us it may have something to do with dyslexia. Did your mother ever tell you if you crawled or didn't?" Nell was mildly dyslexic, and I'd been a help building her confidence in her reading, her writing.

"My mother! Burt, did my mother once sit on the floor with me, and she was my size and I was only as big as this?"

"I imagine so," I said.

"Did she look at me lie in the sun for hours? Was I all she had in the world? I doubt it."

"Antonia's lucky to have you," I said, and I came and sat beside her, and we looked at the baby, squeezing fists and gurgling. In the next night, the baby was gone.

Our empty house is a completely round one. Ever since I'd been walking by it, on my way from school on the top of the hill to my old apartment at the bottom, it had been boarded up, ugly brown shingles peeling and falling, paint peeling away. I thought of living in such an odd round house, tried to imagine how it was laid out inside. A man shoveling his steps next door told me about Mrs. Constantinidis who owned it but lived elsewhere, up the street with her ancient dad. "She hasn't let anybody see it inside for years," he said. "She claims she'll fix it up, move in again someday. I hear there's a staircase in there that would knock your eyes out."

It's one of those Victorian summer houses, not large, along the hillside with a view back toward the city, surrounded by gardens once a hundred years ago before all the lots were filled in with the standard three-family triple-deckers and their chain-link fences. And here is this three-layer decorated wedding cake of a house in their midst. While I stood looking at the arrangement of windows, trying to figure out the plan, a fat little boy rode by on a bike and yelled, "Yeah, man, it's round, it's round, yeah, it's round! The old lady owns it is ca-ray-zee!" I decided I'd go talk to Mrs. Constantinidis.

After we worked out our arrangement, I ended up hiring Liam McGee to help me start fixing it. That was his senior year. He wasn't mine, or Paula's, and he wasn't even finishing school. I didn't need to be a teacher to him anymore, but still I thought a bit before deciding it would be all right to have him working with me. He liked the idea, and soon he was calling me Burt.

In the late spring, when it was sunny and dry again, we put up ladders and started peeling the asphalt shingles off, not knowing how the wood would be underneath, pleased to find most of it was all right. Liam would lean out crazily to reach as far as he could before climbing down and moving the ladder over. I liked working with him, worrying about him, talking back and forth around the curve of the house.

"Burt, how can you stand Mrs. Innocenzo for a friend?" he asked me once from his ladder.

"You think she's keeping you from graduating," I said.

"If it hadn't been for last year, and she could've helped me make it up—"

"If it hadn't been Paula, it would've been someone else, Liam."

"If it hadn't been my mom going in there and fucking around—"

"Well, we know your mom—"

"But, Burt, why do you have to be friends with Mrs. Innocenzo?"

"Paula's one person I can talk to up there," I said. "She's not set against you. She's on your side as much as I am."

"You and her talking to each other in the hall, going off for coffee—it's like you don't care what she did last year to me." He was vehemently pulling shingles off.

"Careful of the boards," I said. "You know, Liam, I need friends too. I can't always keep company with kids, dropping by when they feel like it. Who am I going to go talk to?"

It wasn't an admission I felt I wanted to make. I had told myself I wouldn't seem lonely to him, I wouldn't seem as if I needed anything. Liam had an eye for what people seemed to need. That's how he found his way in. I see him in shorts and sneakers, skinny waist and bony shoulders getting the first pink of the season, hanging off his ladder by a hand, working his face in a tight little fury, ripping off the shingles.

This was the time Frank Innocenzo was getting the Soliloquy

printed. It didn't do Liam much good to think of his younger friend's accomplishments. Frank had some friends who ran a small press called the Spondee out of a bookstore in the city. Mostly they printed thin books of poetry, bound with Florentine paper and illustrated with his woodcuts, signed Francesco I. He did the frontispiece for the Soliloquy, a swirl of flame colored like dried blood, illustrating the opening pages, the pages about fire.

After a faculty meeting, Paula and I met Frank downtown at a Brew 'n' Burger near the bookstore so I could pick up a box of Soliloquies. It'd taken much longer than promised, and the author seemed to doubt the whole business, figured it was just Mr. Stokes and Mrs. Innocenzo trying to encourage him, saying they were getting him published.

He'd told me he didn't actually care much. He was working on something else now. "It's very nice of you," he said, "but I can't get too excited. Who'd want to read it? No one's heard of me."

"Don't think about it," I said. "They'll sit on a shelf at the Spondee, a few other cubbyhole bookstores where Mr. Innocenzo's friends work, or friends of the Spondee people, and at their other store down in Providence. Somebody will pick one up. I'll bring you a box of them when they're ready."

"I'm not going to think about it," he said. He looked at me with a slight smirk, half pleased, half discounting everything. "I'll bring you what I'm working on, if you have time," he said as he edged to the door.

"I want to see it," I said.

He looked back across the empty desks to me. "I don't think Mrs. Innocenzo thinks as much of my writing as you do. She likes it, but she sees what's wrong more."

"Is it useful to talk to her?" I asked, jealous a bit.

"In a different way. I know I have to talk to her too, but I like to talk more to you."

After each short talk with him, in the end, I felt good. Even in his worst times he made me feel good when I talked with him. How can someone do that who is going through bad things himself?

Frank gave me my own copy. Holding the book in my hands, I almost hoped it might have been dedicated to me, but I quickly flipped past the dedication page and saw the letters of a longer name than mine there. The book was fatter than most Spondee books, sixty-two pages, the number of the year of his birth. I had read most of it before, but not in sequence, not at a sitting, and here it all was.

"A few misprints, I'm afraid," said Frank. "See, here it reads 'had loves' instead of 'had loved.' Nothing serious."

"What will he think of it, Burt?" Paula asked when our burgers arrived and I had put the book aside to keep my sticky fingers off it.

"It'll make him happy, but not in a way he'll show," I said.

"I think he'll be embarrassed," said Paula, "and want to keep it to himself."

"This kid is not your average kid," said Frank. "I mean, does he have fights in the hall or kick anybody down stairs or what?"

"This kid slips through as if you didn't see him, Frank," I said. "Other kids don't bother him."

"I don't know how he does it," Paula said, biting into her fat burger. "Frank, remember that kid they call Ladro, the one we saw hanging out on the library steps with that pretty, skinny, freckly girl? I saw Ladro barreling down the hall, slamming people the way he does, and then I heard him say, 'Hey, Og!' and he stopped dead and smiled, and they went off side by side talking whole sentences. Ladro talking whole sentences!"

"I was beat on by every shit in school when I was a kid," said Frank.

I remembered a thing I'd forgotten. "Actually, Paula, there was once," I said, "when I saw this Og of ours in a terrible fight with Liam McGee on the steps in the gym, a year ago, I think, when you were flunking Liam. By the time I got there they'd pulled apart and were walking off in different directions. I saw drops of blood on the steps. I didn't go after either one of them. Later Liam told me he didn't think they were going to be friends anymore."

"And Liam told me back then," said Paula, looking at me firmly, knowing what Liam's case meant to me, "how they'd always been best friends when they were growing up, and now it was the way everything else was going for Liam that spring, he was losing everything, flunking everything, didn't want to be at home, at school, anywhere. He wanted to be out on the streets downtown where no one knew him, fuck it, he said. His usual line of excuses. I said all I wanted was for him to do a minimal amount of work and stop saying fuck in front of me."

"You know, Burt, this Liam was a pain in the ass for Paula last year."

"Don't I know, Frank," I said. I wiped my fingers carefully and picked up the book again in its mottled brown cover. I kept having to look at it.

"Nice job, isn't it," said Frank.

I turned the pages filled with familiar words. "Is it to his mother's memory, Clara Ognissanti, that name on the dedication page, Paula?"

"That sounds right. Clara. So he didn't dedicate his book to his pa as well—"

"Does he tell you anything about them, Paula, or what happened to them?"

Frank was trying to get a waitress's attention for another beer.

"He won't talk about his parents," Paula said. "I did ask about Elsa though. He said she'd asked him in a letter if he had Miss McCune. He wrote her that Miss McCune was Mrs. Innocenzo now. I asked if Elsa married the kid she used to go out with, Martin Keeney, remember him, earnest sort of kid? He used to follow her around, totally dedicated, he'd do anything for her. They got married, he told me, and they moved out to Oregon right after high school."

"Want another beer, Burt?" Frank asked now that he had the waitress there.

"I'll have one," said Paula. But I thought I should get the books to their author early, while the Saint Vincent Home would still open its doors to me. I'd never been there, but Paula was sure it was all right for me to take them to him there.

On the city bus from downtown I held the box on my lap, feeling it was the most substantial thing I'd ever held. I wanted to open it and look at them all, identical copies of the book I was the first ever to see a line of. It wasn't two years since I'd put some of those pages casually in my folder for the weekend.

I changed to a bus that took the avenue along the back side of the hill. I walked up to the street where the Home was. It was a quiet night with a soft rain I couldn't see. These streets were dark—pale, infrequent street lamps, television-blue glows in windows.

After blocks of three-deckers came a cold dark church and then several blocks more and, across the street right up against the sidewalk, a long brick building with high small windows on the first floor, eaves hanging down heavy over the second-floor windows, and five skinny third-floor dormers, and then chimneys. The yellow of low-watt bulbs shone in each window, the same dim light, and over the front door, hanging from the peak of the little archway I stood under, was a bare dim bulb. Holding the box of books, I felt unsettled. This is where he lived, all the time, where he slept at night, and where he wrote.

I pushed a rusty buzzer and then tapped the iron knocker. I waited for a minute and tapped again. I couldn't hear anything in the building, but it wasn't late and all the lights were on. I pushed the buzzer again. The door suddenly opened. A short man in a soutane stood in stocking feet on maroon linoleum.

"I have something to deliver to one of your boys," I said.

"Come in, please. I'm Brother Nor."

I came into a narrow hallway that ran the breadth of the building, a staircase at each end and a double swinging door before me. "It's for Anthony Ognissanti. I don't know if he's told you about his book."

"His devotional writing," said Brother Nor. "Yes, of course."

"I suppose it is, in a way. I'm his teacher—"

"Mr. Innocenzo."

"Mr. Stokes," I said.

"Mr. Stokes, from last year, yes, of course. I couldn't remember. Anthony's our only boy at public high school. Of course, he'd already started when he lost his parents. He does seem to manage quite well there."

I didn't know if I should hand him the box, or if he would let me present it myself. I looked up the hall at one staircase.

"Well, here he is," Brother Nor said, and I turned and looked the other way. There was Anthony on the top stair, just in sight.

"Mr. Stokes?" he asked.

"Come down, Anthony, your book is here," said Brother Nor.

"My book?" He was in his socks too, and his other sweater, the dark blue one with the left-elbow hole.

"Ten copies of it," I said.

He came down fast, socks flopping on the stairs, and he almost slid down the linoleum to us. He seemed smaller, younger, than at school. He didn't take the box but looked at it and then at Brother Nor.

"I had hoped there'd be copies," Brother Nor said. "We wanted one for Monsignor, and for the library at the church. And one for our little library here, I hope."

"And one for you, Brother Nor," said Anthony.

If Brother Nor hasn't read the Soliloquy yet, I thought, he's in for surprises, and God only help the Monsignor.

"We're very interested in Anthony's work," Brother Nor said. "We've never had a boy like him here." I felt I should probably make a gesture toward the door, but Brother Nor said, "You'll excuse me, Mr. Stokes. I'm in the middle of a tutoring session. Thank you so much for bringing Anthony's books." As I said good-bye, he slipped through the swinging doors.

"Take a look," I said to Anthony. I held the box while he slit the tape and opened the four flaps. He reached in and pulled out the stack of brown books. I couldn't tell how he felt. He looked at the top one seriously, looked at the frontispiece, the title page, at the dedication, at the first page of text. I held the empty box and watched his eyes shift across the lines.

"One copy for me," he said, holding the top one to his sweater, and then flipping through the others he said, "and these two can go to our libraries, and this is for Monsignor, and this is for Brother Nor, and I'll send this one to my grandmother even if she doesn't know English, probably just as well, and this to my sister, and then three more, hmmm—one for you, Mr. Stokes."

"Oh, I have my own." I pulled it out of my coat. "But I'd like an autograph from the author. I just happen to have a pen here," I said, smiling.

He put my copy on top of his stack and signed his name inside the cover in his familiar strokes, but thin now, using my extra-fine ballpoint. "Maybe I should add something else?" he asked.

"Just say: For Burt," I said.

"Burnt?" He looked at me, almost afraid.

"B-u-r-t, Burt. You should call me Burt. I'm not your teacher now. I call you Anthony, you call me Burt. Mr. Stokes seems funny."

He looked at me with a slight tilt of his head, wrote For Burt above his name, and looked at me again.

"Thank you," I said, holding my book again.

"Does Mrs. Innocenzo have one?"

"She has two," I said.

"I should probably give one to Liam McGee. I don't know if he wants one. I hardly see him now. Could you give him one if you ever see him?" I nodded and took the eighth copy. "Ladro wouldn't want one, but Nell, his friend, might. I told her about it once."

"And maybe you should keep the last one for yourself as well," I said.

"Maybe," he said, "to save, if I ever have a kid someday. I'll keep this one safe, in the bottom of my drawer."

A sock-footed chubby boy came charging down the steps Anthony hadn't come from, ran and slid wildly past us on the linoleum, and charged up the other flight.

Anthony gave me his patient, contained smile and said, "I have to go back to work."

I patted his shoulder and said good night. I wanted him to be alone with his book.

Nell was mine that year. Her reading was improving. And now she would have this new book to read, and I would read it with her, and it might make her want to read at last, to read Ladro's friend's book, the friend who could make Ladro stop and listen, talk in sentences.

Did she fall in love with him over his book? Though the words weren't too hard, the sense was. She didn't know if it was a story, or telling about how to live your life, or things you were just supposed to get a feeling from, like a dream. We could have worked with an easier book, but she tried so hard with this one.

She told me she had to know what it meant, she had to. And we'd stay late after school, puzzling.

I didn't know how to give Liam his copy. I knew he would want one, but how could he receive it gracefully? On a painting day, we were in my kitchen turpentining our arms, and he was rubbing white paint splotches off his bare chest and knees too. I'd worn my painting overalls, and I'd been more careful anyway. His copy of the Soliloquy was tucked in a pile of my books on the kitchen table. "Look at all the homework I've got this weekend," I said.

"I'm glad to be done with fucking homework," said Liam.

"Don't be so sure," I said.

"Fuck, Burt, I'm never going back."

"Fuck this, fuck that, Liam, gets monotonous."

"What's the commonest word in the English language, Burt? At least in this town."

"Fuck," I said.

"You got it."

"Someone could throw a match at your legs and blow you up with that turp all over you," I said, shaking a box of kitchen matches at him.

"Try it, Burt," he said and, head down, threw himself at my stomach. Liam loved to tussle.

I tickled his middle till he let go. "Now you got paint off my overalls in your hair, you little asshole, Liam."

"I'm going to go take a shower, give me the turp," and off he went, pounding up the stairs.

That wasn't a time to give him the book, I thought. When will it be a time? I sat on one of the stools I'd bought for the kitchen table and opened his copy. Anthony hadn't written anything in it. I turned to the page I'd been working on that week with Nell.

"Anthony's so smart," she had said.

"He is smart."

"I don't know why he has a friend like Ladro. Ladro thinks he's great, calls him Og."

"How long have you and Ladro been going together?" I asked her.

"He was always a year ahead. When Anthony and him were in

eighth and I was in seventh, that's when I met him. We been going around since. You didn't mind Ladro last year, did you, Mr. Stokes?"

"He's not a bad kid," I said. "The funny part is, Nell—" But it was hard for me to explain. "See, from my view, almost twenty years older—"

"You twenty years older? I thought you were, I don't know, twenty-five or something." Coming from a sophomore girl this could have been flirting, but not from Nell. There wasn't a difference between what she said and what she thought. I could see it in her bright eyes, in the twisting of her neck. It was an effort to say things, and she meant them.

I leaned back in my chair and rolled my sleeves up, which I always seemed to do at some point during our tutoring sessions, and tried to say what I meant about these kids: "Anyway, Nell, it looks different to me. Ladro's tough, I know, and difficult, but I can imagine him a kid a few years back, and also grown up in a few years. For you he's a big loud funny guy and he runs the show. Sometimes you love him and sometimes you'd never like to see him again. For me I know he'll bump into me after he's graduated, and we'll laugh about what a time he used to give me."

We went back to our reading. It was that passage about the unseen grandmothers. There seemed to be about twenty of them, slipping in and out of doors, leaving muffins on windowsills, tucking in blue downy quilts, by dripping candlelight telling half-dreamed stories. And here is a grandmother hanging in a clothes bag in the closet, and another is probably lurking under the stairs.

"What the fuck's that?" said Liam, who'd snuck in dripping wet behind me, my brown bath towel tight at his waist. The book must not have looked like a normal book to him.

"Oh, it's your book," I said. "I forgot to give it to you. It's that writing Anthony's been doing."

"Mine?"

"He wanted to give you a copy. All that writing he does, you know, he got it printed up someplace downtown."

"Where'd he get the bucks for that?" said Liam.

"Probably didn't cost too much," I said, improvising fast, "thin book, paper covers. Maybe his sister or that Martin Keeney she married sent him some money."

"You mean Ogna Santy is going to go around trying to sell the stuff he writes for people to read? Well, I'm fucked!"

"Liam, cut out the fucks, for Christ's sake."

"Don't say Christ to me, man," he said, grabbing my shoulders and shaking them hard. Then, "You mean so that's for me? He's giving it? I don't have to buy it?"

"He knew you wouldn't buy it, Liam, but he wanted you to have one."

"Yeah," said Liam in a sad tone when he picked up the book, leaning the other wet arm on my shoulder. "Spondee. I seen that downtown, that crummy bookstore, sort of shambly. I hang out around that block sometimes. There's a porno store next door, you know. Real nice area." He reached over me and put the book back on the table and looked at the title page with his chin digging into the top of my head. "Soliloquy by Anthony Ogna Santy. Who's he think he is—Romeo?"

"He doesn't expect you to read it, Liam."

"Any good sexy parts?" He tossed the book onto the T-shirt he'd left on the counter and leaned back in the door frame.

"Depends on what you find sexy, Liam," I said, growing a little tired of him.

"I'll tell you one thing, Burt. Anthony's still a virge, at least as far as girls is concerned."

"I thought you weren't going to let on Anthony's private life to me," I said.

"That was when we were friends." Liam sauntered into the hall, up the stairs to comb his hair and put his shorts back on.

Helping me work on the house had made him think of it as partly his. He'd take showers, wander around in a towel, open the fridge for something, take a nap, anything he wanted. I liked him being around, and then I'd get to feeling I didn't. Sometimes when he was there I didn't want him to be, sometimes when he wasn't there I did. He never told me anything ahead of time. I didn't know when he'd suddenly have to go, or when he'd suddenly, unexpectedly, show up.

I realized I could now begin to ask questions about Anthony, but in one way I didn't want to, and I would never ask them all at once. And when I recall what Liam told me, in bits and snatches at first, I hear too much about Liam, who didn't like it when he wasn't the subject and never stuck to talking about anyone else. Everything came back to Liam, reminded him of how it was for him. He didn't have a view of other people.

I knew the remodeling was a project not just for the coming summer but for most of my free time in the next school year. That's even why I started it, needing something like that to do in my life. Mrs. Constantinidis had found a good thing in me. She probably knew it when I first knocked on her door and told her I loved the house.

"Oh, it's not for sale. People keep asking me," she said. "I'm moving back next year with my dad, getting storm windows. Everything's on order."

I asked if she had someone working for her.

"Oh yes, I have my contractor and the carpenters lined up, home-improvement loans from the bank. It's all arranged. I'm sorry."

She's a short woman, a bit chubby, with dark unwrinkled skin and wide eyes, in her late sixties, which makes that dad of hers old indeed. She talked to me in the cold vestibule of the house she lives in up the street. She stood in her doorway. Her curtains were all pulled closed, but over the top of her head I could still see the mess inside, cardboard boxes, newspapers in stacks, pillows out of cases, beer bottles in among the books on the shelves.

I told her she'd just destroyed the daydream I'd always had walking home each day past that boarded-up round house: how I'd somehow manage to get the money together to put down, somehow arrange a mortgage, how I'd work on the place, fix it up the way it once might have been.

"That's just what I want too," she said. "I won't move back until it's the way it was."

I asked if she'd lived there herself, or if her father had, but she didn't make it clear, as though they had intended to but somehow hadn't, almost as if something had prevented them. She didn't look odd, or crazy, perhaps only a little excited, tapping her little fingers on the door frame.

"I brought my dad from Greece a few years back to live with me." That was one thing she said, but she also said, "My dad remembers that house so well, the way it once was."

I asked if there was a chance I might ever see it inside, being interested in old houses.

"I haven't let anybody in for years," she said.

"Not your contractor?"

"Oh no, I haven't let him in. I'm going to call him up. He's very busy right now."

I told her to let me know if she ever changed her plans, and I gave her my most permanent address, the school. A few weeks later, she wrote and asked me to stop by and talk again.

Paula thought the arrangement we worked out was risky for me, but I told her I didn't have anything to lose. For the same rent as my small apartment, I now could live in my favorite of houses, as long as I was fixing it up, and there was still the chance Mrs. Constantinidis would let me buy in. She'd say, "You know, Mr. Stokes, I might consider letting you have it for a nice price, depending how your work turns out. We'll sit down and talk sometime." Or: "I just might be able to deduct your rent and remodeling expenses from the eventual price, Mr. Stokes." But another time she'd say: "They're putting condominiums in that empty schoolhouse across the street. I'll get a top price for my house, if I hold out." Once, when I saw her on the street, carrying her groceries in the grumpiest of moods, she said: "Oh, I ought to burn it down for the insurance!" I never knew what to say. I'd always nod and smile and repeat how much I'd like to buy the house. It still goes on like that now that all but the third floor is done and I've been there over two years. Paula thinks I'm too hopeful, love the house too much, that I can't come out of the arrangement happily.

It did worry me what Mrs. Constantinidis made of Liam. When I'd knocked on her door to report the surprisingly good condition of the wood under the shingles, she asked me, "Who's that boy you have hanging off ladders practically naked? Tell him to get dressed. And I walked by and saw him standing in an open window with nothing on—I mean nothing!"

"He'd probably just taken his shower," I said. "I'll put up curtains, Mrs. Constantinidis."

"This neighborhood doesn't care for bare bottoms," she said, shaking her head at me in her doorway. "People keep curtains closed." She gave me a fierce little tap on the middle of my chest and closed her door.

When I told Liam to be careful where he dried off, he said, "What's the fucking big deal about my ass I'd like to know!"

I did begin to find out more about Anthony, but I did it in a way Liam could take as my showing concern for Liam. I asked why they'd stopped being friends. At first he wouldn't say much. He'd say it was because Anthony was a fuckhead, or because Anthony spent all his time writing. With Nell too, in our reading sessions, I'd asked a question here or there, not to look inquisitive, usually more about Ladro than about his friend Og. When it came to our reading, it was Nell who asked the questions of me: "How can Anthony think up something like this?" or "How can he write all these words?"

"He sits at the Saint Vincent Home and writes, every night," I said. "He doesn't have a family."

"Does he have his own room?" she wanted to know.

I said I thought he did, having walked past the Home again later the night I brought the books and stood across the street and looked at the yellow windows. The shades were drawn on the second floor, and those high first-floor windows only showed the dark paneling of the empty hall. Only the farthest of the dormers had a light in it. There I saw a head of black hair like Anthony's, bent over as if reading at a desk. It looked like a big empty building but for Anthony in it. The soft rain had stopped, and it had gotten windier. I felt restless. Ten o'clock had just passed. As I walked on I did see a light in a side window too, Brother Nor's room, perhaps.

I walked up over the hill of our town—the library, the high school, the town hall in a row on the crest, treeless, windy—and down past the shabby, dim hospital, past my all-night corner store, the lights of downtown, the city, stacked up in tall buildings four miles away, and then to my round house against the night, none of my windows lighted, no one home until I got there. But now, with my wife, with Nell, as I come up the hill at suppertime from my new job, she's there, a light in her bedroom. Only weeks ago there was a light in Antonia's room too, that little room with its curtains closed now, its door always shut.

Will Nell be just mine now, without the baby? Why should she stay here, when she is only just eighteen, when her parents are bound to forgive her, take her back? This is her waiting place, while the feelings die. I keep carefully to myself, not to sway her.

Yesterday evening we walked out, took the narrow streets along the hillside as it grew dark. Then we meandered down, she always on my arm, to the avenue and across it to the Serenata Restaurant, crowded as usual. For decorations they have plastic logs with red lights swirling through them that they've stuck above each booth as light fixtures.

In our booth when we were finished with supper, elbows on our table, we sipped more wine and looked across at each other. They had served her wine too, perhaps because since having the baby she has looked older. We went through our questions again.

"Where is Antonia now, Burt?" she asked.

"I'm sure she's with Elsa. Where could she be if not there?"

"He could've taken her anywhere," she said.

"But where else could she be? We have Elsa's letter. It was her warning. And she says the baby's name should be Clara, the way he would've wanted it, after their mother, not him."

"My baby's Antonia," she said.

"You know that I'm still willing to talk with the police, Nell."

"You've had enough to do with the police," she said.

"But I'll do it," I said. "Why don't you want me to?"

"I'm afraid of you talking with them again," she said. She'd begun to tremble, a shakiness from her elbows up to her thin hands pressing into her cheeks. Tears were coming. I put my hands on the round soft parts of her arms that trembled.

"There are reasons, aren't there, Burt?" She looked deep in my eyes.

"Reasons?"

"Why we shouldn't try to find her."

"There are difficulties," I said.

"Her name is Clara Keeney, she lives somewhere in Oregon, her aunt will love her, she'll have her life there."

I let her arms go, sat back. "We've been through the round again," I said. "We talk, but we don't do anything. We feel bad, we wonder where she is, and then we get round to deciding she is there and she will be happy."

"I have to keep going through the round," said Nell. "Burt?"

"What?"

"What would Anthony want?"

If I told her what he wrote in the last of those Letters Of My Dead Brother, she would know that he wanted Elsa to have the baby. How long can I keep those letters from her? Will someone who knew her come upon them and send them to her, out of cruelty or even innocently, not knowing?

"There isn't an answer," I said. "I just think of his last book, of what he wrote in memory of his old grandmother: 'I never saw her, I will never see her, I always see her.'" I looked at Nell, who was letting tears come out of her eyes.

"We read that last winter by our fire," she said. "I was pregnant and warm. I'd decided to keep the baby, hadn't I, Burt, and you and me'd got married."

There was a waiting line, people eyeing us in our booth, so we left soon. Walking up the hill, Nell was calmer. "Do you remember Martin Keeney?" she asked me.

"I can't picture him anymore in my mind. I can think back to when I was new here and how I was afraid of you Eastern kids I had to teach. I remember being relieved to have Martin speaking up in class, asking me questions while the others were causing trouble. What did he look like?"

"Will Antonia think he's her father?" Nell asked.

"Don't you think they'll tell her?"

"They can tell her anything they want," Nell said. "She won't know anything about what happened. Already she doesn't know anything. Burt, do you think in her mind there's a picture of me leaning down over her?"

"There must be," I said.

"But she won't be able to remember it," said Nell, linking her arm in mine as we paced slowly uphill.

"If she saw you again there'd be a feeling in her," I said, "and maybe if she saw me. Let's go to the police station, Nell, right now, before we think about it."

We kept heading home, Nell's elbow bent tightly around mine. She didn't say a thing more, and I knew not to say anything. She was beginning another trembly spell. She would be silent now, maybe for a day, would shake her head if I tried to ask her questions. She may not even have heard my last sentence. She may have stopped listening when she said Antonia wouldn't be able to remember her. Thinking of her loss, and of her freedom, makes her go like this, I think.

When I come home from work tonight, will she be ready to talk again? I'm staying at work late again using the word processor. These late afternoons I find myself here after the others have left, and then I lock the disc away in my bottom desk drawer overnight. Tonight I want to stay even later than six-thirty.

I called her at six, and she picked up the phone. I said, "Nell, it's me. Are you feeling all right?"

"Burt?" she asked.

"Do you want me to come home? If you're all right, I'll stay awhile and catch up on work. Are you all right? Are you watching television?" I heard it in the background.

"Stay," she said. I asked if she was sure. She said "Stay" again as if she wanted me to stay away, but not as if she was mad.

I thought a few seconds. I told her to call me here if she wanted me. She didn't say anything. I told her, "I'll call you again in a while. I love you, Nell, I worry about you. I'll come right home if you want. You just call, and I'll call in a while anyway."

I heard a murmur. I said good-bye and then I felt I should go home, but I turned on the machine and looked at where I'd left off yesterday, in the middle of a sentence, and here I am typing again and watching my words shine on the screen.

That summer of starting to fix up the round house, two summers ago, I found out from Liam how he and Anthony had grown up near each other and played together on the street. The McGees still live there, down the hill and one block up from the

avenue, but where Anthony's three-decker used to be there is
the blank new five-story project, housing for the elderly. Back
then Elsa used to baby-sit for Liam and his sisters. He said he
liked it when she came over. She'd tell him how much more
mature he was than her little brother. Anthony got in her things,
she'd say, but Liam would just sit on her lap and watch television
while she did schoolwork. I thought of her doing those tedious
compositions for me with a squirmy nine-year-old Liam on her
lap. "You kids' study habits!" I said. Apparently, she'd have her
notebook on the fat arm of the television chair and she'd scribble
a line when inspiration came to her. Liam would slump his head
into her left shoulder and stare at the screen.

She liked to tell him how mean her father was, how he made
her work too hard, how she never liked to be at home, would
much rather sit for the McGees. Liam would get her to give him
a bath after she'd bathed his sisters and put them to bed. "That
was my first turn-on," he told me, "having her scrub my little
butt."

I'd replaced the leaky rusted skylight on the round house with
a Plexiglas one that opened and you could climb onto the flat
roof. Now that it was warm summer and I had weekdays free,
we'd take long noon breaks and lie in the sun up there. We
couldn't be seen, except from the upper windows of the empty
schoolhouse across the street, so Mrs. Constantinidis couldn't
complain about Liam sunning in his red bikini underpants. I'd
pull the straps of my painting overalls off my shoulders and roll
up the pant legs, but I've never been easy about taking off my
clothes.

This was where I got Liam talking. When we worked on
ladders, it was just a shouted comment now and then, usually
with fucking this's and that's. And inside the house, carpentering,
or painting, or having lunch, Liam didn't stay put, unless he was
out cold napping on my bed. Because he went out late downtown
and his parents wouldn't let him loaf around at home, he'd make
up his sleep at my house. When he was awake, he was wriggly
and distracted. I'd get him started stripping wallpaper, and soon
he'd want to sand floors. He never sat at the table to eat but
walked around dropping crumbs.

But on the roof, he'd be stretched out on a towel, and I'd lean up against the chimney and ask him things, offhand.

"Did you lord it over Anthony when you guys were little?"

"He was smaller than me for a while, being younger a year. Then he started getting taller, the fucker. You wouldn't know how it is being small for your age like me."

"What do you know about me as a kid, Liam!" I said.

"You were a bookwormy asshole, I know that."

"I really wasn't," I said. "I was sort of absentminded. I never got things done on time."

"So now you're taking it out on a bunch of helpless kids. I know you, Burt." He'd turn over every five minutes to keep his tan line even, and he got me to spread suntan oil where he couldn't reach in the middle of his back.

"So Anthony was smaller once." I tried to get him back to Anthony.

"He used to do what I wanted," Liam said. "We'd bike around. He'd follow me everywhere. I'd ride no hands, but he wouldn't do that. His dad would come out yelling to get out of the street, get on home. I hated that guy, his dad, what Elsa told me he'd do to her. He'd give her a whack when she didn't do that good in school. He was always getting on her."

"You were her sympathetic listener," I said, finding it hard to imagine.

"Her dad wanted her to be Miss Bookworm. I don't know why. Her mom didn't want her to. Her mom was a night nurse at the hospital, a real lumpy type. I never liked playing there with Anthony. I had him come to my house."

"Was he a quiet kid?" I asked.

"Anthony? He talked all the time. He was a riot. He had languages he'd talk, cat talk, dog talk. He could talk like a duck. I'd crack up. See, he was the crazy one, and I was the serious one, the one he followed around. Can you believe I was the serious one? Me!"

"You have your serious side, Liam. It gets me impatient with you when you don't give yourself credit."

"And that's what you tell your pal Paula. 'Oh, yeah, Paula, that crazy kid Liam McGee, he's got a real serious side, you got to give him credit."

"Forget it, Liam. I'm not going to go on arguing that."

I looked out over the peaked shingled rooftops, the slate mansards, the flat tarred roofs of the warehouses on the avenue. There was the blank cube of elderly housing, pinkish brick like pale old skin. I sipped my midday beer to cool off. When we climbed down inside he'd drink the whole pitcher of ice water in the fridge, but on the roof Liam liked to get as dehydrated as he could, dripping sweat and shining from it.

Once he told me this story: "Anthony'd get me in trouble all the time, being crazy. He'd say the Our Father in his duck voice, and I'd take a fit laughing. And you think he's such a bookwormy little good Catholic orphan! He was a little fuck. We were on our bikes going around once. His father worked maintenance at the town hall. Anthony knew how to get in the side door, down the basement. He starts flipping switches. Any switch he sees, he flips it. On things go off, off things go on. Not just lights, but like furnaces, elevators, fuse boxes. I'm following him through these dark tunnels. The idea's to run through and out the other end before anyone upstairs figures it out. We hear someone coming. I'm banging into things. I'm so fucking scared. 'Put up your hood,' says Anthony in his duck voice. We zoom out the other end door, and somebody's leaning out the window upstairs, like the mayor's office, yelling after us. 'This way, follow me!' says the duck, and we scoot around the building and get out of there. The only thing they see is the color of our hoods. I didn't wear that parka the rest of the winter. My mom thought I was crazy going around in two sweaters."

"The Anthony I know did that?" I asked.

"Burt, you have to know, Anthony was a little fuck till his parents died. All right, don't believe me." He flipped over, adjusting his waistband to check his tan line, and said, "I sure am getting to be Mr. Bronzola."

I told him to remember how fair skin burns.

Liam liked talking about Elsa more than Anthony. He told me he got sulky when Martin Keeney was around. "She wasn't supposed to, but she had him come by our house when she was sitting for my sisters. She wasn't sitting for me anymore, she was more like my friend. When she got my sisters to bed, she'd call up Martin, and he'd be right over. I loved it before, when she'd just talk about this guy she liked. She'd get real explicit, if you know what I mean. It got me all turned on, sitting in the kitchen having a snack and her telling me about feeling each other up. I didn't like it when he actually came by, though. He thought I was just a kid she was sitting for. He didn't know I knew how big his dick was and how he loved to get his head up her dress when they were in the backseat of somebody's car."

"All right, Liam—"

"He was such a fuck to think I didn't know what was on his mind, Burt. Then once, Burt, see, let me just tell you this—"

I tried to look perturbed and indifferent.

He leaned up on one elbow, looked right at me and said, "Well, once, I just went off to bed early, but didn't really, and I knew I could watch them through the radiator grate between our hall and the living room. I was kneeling there in my PJ's, and it's just like she told me, she's on the couch with her legs spread and I can't see his head because it's under her dress. I just see her face going all crazy, and he's got his big dick out of his pants with his hand and pounding away on it." Liam turned on his back again, arching and stretching, pleased with himself.

I began to think I was going to be in a bad situation with Liam sometime, and it made me want to talk about Anthony again, get away from this lolling around. I looked across at the blank upper windows of the schoolhouse, not at Liam anymore. "Where were your parents all these nights?" I asked.

"My mom, she has all these meetings, ward committee, ladies' church group. That's how she is—I've told you. My dad, it's just bowling with him, bowling, bowling. He's only assistant manager at his office, you know."

I wanted to see Anthony that summer too, but how could I? I decided to phone the Home, and I spoke to Brother Nor, who said Anthony was away for a month. He'd taken the bus across the country to Oregon to visit his sister.

"All alone?" I asked. I could see him on a bus, in some rear seat squeezed in next to a fat lady, with his notebook on his lap, writing.

"He's quite self-sufficient," said Brother Nor. "Is this the teacher who brought the books? Is it Mr. Innocenzo?"

His same mistake. I told him it was Mr. Stokes, and suddenly I feared Brother Nor was about to let me have it for leading Anthony astray.

"Mr. Stokes," he said, "I want you to know how moved we've been by Anthony's work. He wouldn't tell you that. He'd say in his usual way that we'd seemed to like it. But, of course, it's more than that. Of course, it's a strange book, and that takes adjusting to. All I'd seen before, you see, were little snippets he'd shown me, and I didn't have a sense of the whole. Little parables and homilies they seemed to be—the comforting vision of the grandmothers, or that frustrating conversation of animals who don't speak the same language—but when it came to the whole, frankly, I had no idea it would be so much a continuous elaborated vision, so much a meditation outward, don't you think, nothing self-absorbed about it." Brother Nor seemed hopeful of launching a serious discussion with me. "Anthony has such a clear-seeing mind," he went on, "not learned, of course, by no means, not yet, but what might he not go on to do? That's what thrills us."

"The Monsignor is thrilled too?" I asked, still cautious.

"I might not have been sure," said Brother Nor, "but after you brought the copies and I sat up late in my room with mine—"

"But didn't the Monsignor expect it to be, I think you called it, devotional writing?"

"And what else is it, Mr. Stokes?"

"I wouldn't know what to call it. A soliloquy, loneliness, desperation—"

"We went to the church the next afternoon," said Brother Nor. "Anthony does custodial work for Monsignor, sweeping and cleaning. Monsignor saw us in his cold tall stone office. He'd told me earlier not to worry how he'd take Anthony's work. Nothing Anthony did could shock him. He told me, 'After all, he's been through the fire, Brother Nor.' So I told him here was Anthony with a copy of his little book for him. 'And one for the library, if you want it,' said Anthony, not the least apprehensive. Of course Monsignor would want it for the library, and how kind of Anthony to have a copy for him too! So I stood back and watched, Anthony in front of the desk, Monsignor standing behind it with the book in his hands. He was reading the page about the moths."

"It's about masturbation!" I said, realizing at the same time I shouldn't be saying it.

"Ah, perhaps so," said Brother Nor, amused with me.

I remember going over that page with Nell. She especially liked it, but I kept hoping she wouldn't think about it too much, which she didn't. But there was that window of his at night, his lone dormer, and the little soft wings beating against his screen in warm weather, and there he was sitting at his desk before it, looking up at the white things shining on the screen, and the words took on a rhythm of beating and fluttering. He wrote moth words that meant, "Let me in," "Open to me," "I have to need you," and with his own pen strokes he told them, "Stay in the night," "You must not come," "Even if you die there."

"Do you suppose that Monsignor is unacquainted with the uses of metaphor?" Brother Nor asked me over the phone.

I tried to sound amused myself. "Perhaps I'm too careful with clergymen, but to call it devotional writing—" I was feeling somewhat condescended to.

I heard Brother Nor breathe deep at the other end of the phone, he on his side of the hill, I silent on mine. "I can't explain it, Mr. Stokes. Perhaps it's a quality Anthony's taken on because of what happened to his parents. Most of our boys, of course, were orphaned at an earlier age. And the fact that his sister didn't want him out there with her then, and he came to us—"

"And this dear sister of his he's visiting now—" I said, suddenly angry at everybody.

"They'll be friends again," said Brother Nor. "The bad feelings are dying. They'll have a clear course before them."

I found myself asking Brother Nor if Anthony ever fought with other boys at the Home.

"Well, I certainly recognized the pages about a struggle on the stairs," he said, still amused. "And Monsignor did too. I watched him hold the book closer and purse his lips. Anthony rested a hand on the desk quite confidently. I stood behind, thinking how we must darn that elbow hole, when Monsignor said, 'And this is when you first came to us, Anthony, I see,' and went on to recall how Anthony had pushed a little boy down the stairs because he was running too much in the halls, and he cut his knee and there was blood. But Anthony explained how he'd changed it in his Soliloquy to be about two dogs who each wanted the other one to do what he wanted to do, and they're trying to decide whether to go up or down, and when they fight on the hillside they think they hate each other for a moment. That part about the one going off and lifting his leg, he said, was put in to be a little funny. He guessed Monsignor didn't mind. Monsignor laughed and told him they'd sit down and talk sometime soon when he'd studied the book. So, Mr. Stokes, it's not as you feared. May I even say a thanks to you, because I believe it was in your class, wasn't it, he began to write these pieces?"

It made me feel better that Brother Nor didn't know the dog fight was really the fight with Liam. So I thanked him too, gave him my number, and asked if he might have Anthony call me when he got back from the west.

"I wouldn't mind a bus trip," said Liam after I told him where Anthony was. "I'd get the fuck out of here. Why should I stay around?"

"I hope you'll help me finish the job first," I said.

"Your job is going on forever, Burt." He looked somewhat disgusted with me. This time he was lying on his stomach, his cheek pressed flat on the brown towel. "I want to go to the fucking west, or the south where it's always hot like this and I can just lie around and fucking do nothing."

I always stopped caring about him when he started up his line, and because I was tired of him as could be that muggy noontime and the only thing before me was an afternoon of steaming off wallpaper and Liam roaring the sander across the floors, I decided to ask the question that for all this time I hadn't quite wanted to ask yet about what happened to Anthony's parents.

But before I could ask him, Liam raised his cheek from the towel, stretched out one arm pointing down the hill and began to tell me what I wanted to know. "See that ugly pink building down there, that big square one? You know what that is?"

I told him I did.

"That's where one of my grandmothers lives now. It's a project. That's her window, top one on the right. I guess I told you who used to live where it is."

"The Ognissantis," I said.

"Why do you say Own-ye-SAWN-tee? It's Ogna Santy, for Christ's sake!"

"Americanized Italian sounds awful," I said.

"You know where you get this Own-ye-SAWN-tee? Probably Mrs. Innocenzo."

"She's Irish, like you, Liam. Anthony says Ognissanti himself."

"Not to me. But I suppose now that he's Mr. Romeo Soliloquy—"

"What were you going to say about the Ognissantis?"

"It would've been something to see their fire from up here," Liam said. I knew it was something about a fire. "You knew about their fire, didn't you, Burt?"

"I knew something about it," I said. I leaned back against the chimney and stared at the skin-pink building, thinking how Anthony's book began, the pages about fire. Liam hadn't flipped onto his back but had put his cheek back down against the towel, and a sad look had come into his eyes.

"I could tell you some things Anthony made me never tell anyone," he said, "but I can tell you because I'm going to get the fuck out of here and he won't see me again."

"You shouldn't tell me a secret, Liam."

"It's not secret. It'd be my secret as much as his. He's just scared, and I'm not. You wouldn't tell, Burt. See, I trust you. You think I don't, but I do."

"I know you do," I said, but I wasn't sure if it was just to get me to listen to what he wanted to tell me that he said that, or if something was really coming out of Liam then. I felt my boredom with him lifting, in case it was. "Tell me what you want to," I said.

He looked straight into the towel and talked in a muffled way: "Oh, he was just spending the night at my house. My sisters were sleeping at our grandmother's where she used to live over the hill.

Mom and Dad were out late. My room's behind our kitchen, so I wheeled the TV around into my room, and we got crackers and cookies and we were looking at shows in bed. We were going to split the mattress and the spring so as he'd sleep on the floor when my parents came, but then we were wrestling around on the bed, and he was such a horny little fucker he didn't seem too worried when we started fooling around like that. I don't want to tell you about it, but you get the idea, Burt—everybody does it sometime. So we were doing things like that, and we didn't hear sirens a couple blocks down. It started in the wiring. They had the top floor, and they didn't get out. So that's where Anthony was when it happened."

"Elsa?" I said without thinking, I was so confused.

"No, Elsa was married, Burt, she'd left way back. This was just a couple years ago, you know. I was in your fucking class already. That's when everything started going wrong."

"It wasn't till your year with Paula—"

"Fuck," said Liam, and I saw him crying onto the towel, "I tried a whole year then wanting to help Anthony, when he had nothing, and Elsa thought it was his fault for not being at home that night, but she was gone out of here anyway and having troubles of her own out there. I'm sure that cuntsuck Martin Keeney wanted to keep his head up her dress in private anyway, no kid brother sneaking around. And I wanted to be Anthony's friend still. I even tried to get my parents to adopt him, or be made guardians, but he went to the Saint Vincent Home, and we didn't get together much, he was so afraid I'd want to touch him again or tell Ladro about it, and he told me he'd be my friend still but I'd better never try it with him again. It wasn't the same. Someone had to hold him and touch him. I can't help it if I'm fucking perverted. This whole thing is fucked. And the next year he told me you were his best new teacher, and he started writing all that stuff for you, and I was just horny as hell and going off downtown around that block I told you about, getting myself sucked off and you name it. And Innocenzo starts giving me a hard time. Don't you get it!"

He sat up, looked at me through tears, and swung his brown legs over the open skylight. He let himself down the ladder, and then I heard him going down the stairs and a door slam on the second floor. I stared at the brown towel with his sweat on it, then I rolled down my pant legs, pulled my overalls onto my shoulders, picked up the beer bottle, the bottle of suntan oil and the wet towel and let myself down the ladder to see what I could do. I felt my time of being carefully alone was coming to an end.

Colloquy

Nell is no better. She hadn't eaten when I came home last night after all that writing. She was in her room, where we keep the television, staring at it. I brought her beef stew and some bread, which she hardly ate. I came in again to get her tray and asked if she wouldn't eat more than that. She shook her head. "Would you smile at me?" I asked. She looked at me and gave a smile, but one she was holding back. It lasted only a second. I took the tray.

I ate something myself, in the kitchen with my bowl and mug, breadcrumbs sprinkling across the table. I thought about the disc in its unlabeled slipcase locked in my drawer at work with The Letters Of My Dead Brother. I wanted to keep it going, but I thought I'd better not stay so late again. Nell gets further down without me, but when I'm there and she comes out to the bathroom and sees me through the door across the landing, propped up in bed reading, she knows she has me, and in a few days she feels up to talking again, to being together. I'll just spend a short time after work each afternoon, but then I'll go home to her.

People here at the office find me odd. I don't have a Paula to talk to on breaks. I have a coffee and go back to my desk, and since they know I'm married they don't ask me over after work to meet a nice friend of theirs. When the baby was born, they chipped in and bought me one of those papooses for carrying babies, the standard office baby gift. It was taken along with Antonia. On my desk I put a picture of her, newborn, and they all admired her, and they still ask politely how she's doing. How can I tell them that she's gone, and it's not been in the papers or on the radio and I'm going about my work as if everything at home is safe?

"I hope your wife strolls by with Antonia sometime now it's warm weather," said Faye when she brought me some forms to sort through this morning. Could I get Elsa to send me a new picture of Antonia to help me keep up my fiction? I know that's where she is, at Elsa's, some town by the ocean in Oregon, but she wouldn't let me have evidence like that. Does she walk by the ocean with Antonia in that papoose? My feeling for what it's like out there comes more from what Anthony wrote when he came back than from his snapshots: a wide flat stretch of sand, and wind, and water much too cold for your ankles.

Anthony must have come back early in August, but he didn't call me. By then, because of Liam, I was even a little afraid of his call. I did get a call, though, from the man who is now, on paper, my father-in-law. I didn't recognize the name until he repeated it.

"Parshall, Nell Parshall's father."

"Mr. Parshall, hello." He'd caught me in the shower. I'd grabbed a towel but was dripping now on the bedroom floor. The ring had woken Liam from one of his naps. He sat up on the bed and looked over at me half asleep. I held the receiver between my ear and shoulder and toweled myself as best I could while I listened.

"They wrote us Nell isn't staying in the faster track this fall," Mr. Parshall said in a tired voice. "See, we wanted her to have Mrs. Innocenzo because we hear she's best."

I told him it was an administrative decision teachers didn't have control over.

"But, see, she was in the faster track last year."

"And she was doing well," I said, "but I had to do extra work with her, and the school's not set up for that kind of tutoring. I did it because Nell's smart, Mr. Parshall. Her reading problem doesn't have anything to do with her smartness. It just slows her down. But the trouble is, if I tutor Nell, it looks bad if I don't tutor others. The administration asked that I not keep special kids after class. I've got three big groups of kids to worry about. I went to a small rural school, Mr. Parshall, where teachers looked out for you, but it's not the same here, I've had to learn."

"I appreciate what you're saying," he said and went on to propose, in a voice that sounded dull to the idea, that he could pay me for tutoring sessions, so Nell would keep liking school.

"But I don't think I can get her switched to Mrs. Innocenzo," I said.

"I appreciate that," said the dull voice, "but, see, Nell did so good with you, and we want her to keep liking school for once."

So we arranged it, and when he asked my rates I didn't know what to say, so we went back and forth a bit and settled on five dollars a session.

"Only five!" said Liam. "You really know how to be had, Burt." I sat down on the edge of the bed, and he leaned over and started rubbing my shoulders quite hard.

This was also how we'd got started, but the other way around, after he told me about the fire, when I came down and found him on my bed, still a bit chokey. I'd rubbed his shoulders for a while to calm him, and it wasn't a surprise when he pulled my arms around him and started licking them, my forearms, inside my elbows, where the veins are on my wrists, on the backs of my hands. Then quickly, it was back to tussling, and he was getting my overalls off.

He still disappeared most evenings, maybe to check in with his family, or go off downtown, I didn't know what, but it didn't concern me. Then he'd drop by again next morning. We'd start to work for a bit, but we couldn't keep from grabbing at each other, and it always led to sex, in some form. Then if it was sunny, I'd have a sandwich and beer on the roof and he'd keep up his tan, and then we'd come down and he'd nap while I read beside him, and we might have a little sex again when he woke up, or maybe we'd do some more work on the house. The days had begun to seem the same to me. I didn't feel that anything was happening.

Paula and Frank came back in mid-August from Frank's summer artist commune. I had a drink one evening with Paula at the Brew 'n' Burger while Frank was checking in with the Spondee people. I half expected to see Liam drift by the window and felt odd about it. Would it embarrass him to be seen out on the prowl? I knew it would make him mad to see me with Paula. He'd forgotten her that summer and stopped all that furious talk, he'd forgotten Anthony, and school. He was starting his new life.

"Have you seen Anthony's latest work?" Paula asked me as soon as we sat down.

"He was going to show me something new in the spring, but then he told me he had revisions to make, and then he went off to Oregon."

"Yesterday I saw him at the library," said Paula, "when I went to pay my summer reading fines. He was on the steps talking to that girl of Ladro's."

"By the way, Paula, I'm in a little trouble at school for tutoring that girl."

"They never know when they have a good thing, do they," said Paula.

"But you saw Anthony—"

"There he was. He looked great, relaxed, not so skinny, a bit taller. What a great kid! I think he's interested in that girl, Burt. Ladro won't have a prayer once Anthony gets moving."

"She doesn't know what to make of Anthony," I said, and I told Paula how I was using the Soliloquy for my tutoring.

"I think his days of soliloquizing are past," said Paula. "He's gone on to a Colloquy now."

I wondered how he'd come upon a word like that. Paula said she thought he'd been spending time with the dictionary lately. They'd gone into the library together and xeroxed some of his new notebook for her. "I'll show it to you, Burt."

"Better if I wait for him to show it to me," I said, trying to remind myself that Anthony had said he liked talking to me more than to Paula. "I don't want to have to pretend I haven't seen it when I have."

"Well, you're going to be surprised. The animals are gone—"

"And that lonely watcher, who never touches anything but his own bones, as he puts it—"

"Anthony's changing, Burt. I don't mean it's not still dreamlike, but it's not just inside Anthony. He's seeing from outside himself." Paula looked over at me proudly, as though we both had a stake in Anthony's progress, both had had to do with effecting it. It had been weeks since I'd given Anthony so much thought, and I was almost having trouble concentrating on him. Then Paula said, "Burt, you seem restless."

"I feel like I'm calm," I said, but she reached across and took my hand to steady it. "It's probably the round house," I said. "The work's slowed down. It's almost time for school, and there's so much to do."

"Did you scrape the horrible wallpaper off?"

"Yes, but it's still a mess, and we haven't even started upstairs."

"We?"

"Liam—" I began, realizing how far back I'd have to start if I were ever to try to tell her.

"He stuck with it all summer? I was sure you'd have him a week, if that."

"He's out of that way of thinking, Paula, and every third word isn't even fuck anymore."

"Burt, you do good things with kids. Here I go fighting them down to the bone, and you just talk to them and they love you. Have I impressed on you how much Anthony talks about you? Mr. Stokes said this, Mr. Stokes said that. You should ask him soon to show you his new work. I think he's a little reticent, as if he shouldn't ask because what you give him is so valuable he shouldn't expect to get it often. That's how he thinks. Whereas he can talk to Mrs. Innocenzo any old day."

As Paula said all this, I was looking into my beer at the bubbles in the gold. Why had I set Anthony to the side, stopped thinking of what it was like talking to him? I kept looking into my beer. It seemed like a treasure warming in my hands. "I was afraid I pressed him too much," I said.

"Remember, he's a boy without a father," said Paula.

We were quiet for some seconds, and then I said, "His mother and his father burned to death in a fire when he was fourteen."

"So that's what it was," said Paula.

"Liam told me. Anthony was spending the night at the McGees'."

"Christ."

"Apparently the McGees were out, and they came home late and saw the fire trucks and woke up the boys, Liam said, and Anthony ran down the street in the middle of the night barefoot, terrified, in his underwear."

"Oh, Christ, Burt."

"I can't imagine it," I said. "When I think of my mother and father out there, safe and old—"

"And Elsa didn't take him?"

"It's hard to get a consecutive story from Liam. I think Elsa's turned out a little odd. Liam says she blamed Anthony for not being there. The fire started in the living room where he used to sleep on the couch. She thinks if he'd been there that night he would've noticed it in time and gotten them out. Liam says at the funeral home she wouldn't talk to Anthony. She arrived straight from her flight, and Liam saw her come up to Anthony and shake him by the shoulders and scream at him, 'Why weren't you there!' and she cried the rest of the time and hardly talked. 'Send him to San Marino to our grandmother,' Liam heard her tell someone. She didn't talk to her old pal Liam she used to baby-sit for. Martin hadn't come with her. She was alone, no other relatives in this country at all. What's touching, Paula, is Liam wanted his parents to adopt Anthony, or be his guardians."

"You're fonder of Liam than you used to be, Burt," said Paula. "You don't sound exasperated with him."

"He's a good kid, really," I said, and then a thought I'd been having without knowing it came out of my mouth: "But I don't think he's ready to show it. He still wants to get into some kind of bad trouble."

Paula looked up at me, thinking, over the lip of her beer glass.

"I mean he's not over it yet. I'd been thinking that he was, but I suddenly have a feeling that he really isn't."

Our conversation went on to the various other students I regularly discussed with Paula, to our colleagues and what they'd

been up to, to Frank's work and how Paula had had a relaxing
summer reading and was readier than I was for school to begin. I
kept finding my eyes glancing at the window, expecting a glimpse
of the sleeveless blue T-shirt Liam had been wearing that afternoon.
I wondered why it had come out that I was afraid for him, but I
suppose it was because I'd remembered how much I wanted to
see and talk to Anthony, to teach him, in fact, and now that Paula
had told me how he valued me, I knew I had it in me to grow
tired of Liam again. For all the hours of tangling our bodies
together that summer, I could grow tired of him.

Frank came in, brown and bearded, full of enthusiasm. "Burt
Stokes, it's you again," he said. "Hey, we missed you."

"Good to see you, Francesco." I never thought about Frank,
but then he seemed comforting as he slid in next to Paula.

"Big stuff's afoot," he said. "Burt, you know the Trochee, our
Providence branch? Well, branch is a little grandiose—can you
see it, a whole chain of cubbyholes! Anyway, they're going to
want me down there a couple evenings. And I'll distribute too,
which means I get the van, Paula."

"You're not going to be spending nights down there?" Paula
asked, picking at the hairs on his arm.

"Worried I'll take to cavorting?"

"I didn't know the Spondee was such an operation," I said.

"Kitchell's got his grand design, forming a distributing
cooperative," said Frank. "That's why I'll do my stint on the
road. It doesn't pay only to peddle Spondee books, but if I peddle
a whole van full of other small-press books all over New England,
college bookstores, trendy suburban bookstores, artsy-fartsy
bookstores, and then we connect with a West Coast guy and a
Mid-Atlantic guy, and I suppose even a Midwest guy, eh, Burt, if
they got bookstores in the Midwest—"

I raised an eyebrow. This was the one little standing joke
between us.

"And then we get someone who'll cover the South—" Frank
leaned forward on his elbows and began whispering: "And the
other thing is, Kitchell doesn't want me talking about this yet, but
he's starting a sideline that could support our whole operation."

"The collected works of Anthony Ognissanti," I said.

"No, no, something with a bit more sleaze."

Paula puffed out her cheeks and huffed. "Is this what you and Kitchell were joking about, and I just thought it was all a joke?"

"No, no, no, but I mean elegant, I mean a little elegant erotica, the sort of thing you're not ashamed of on the bedside table."

"Not my bedside table, pal," said Paula.

"No, actually, Kitchell's been talking to one of the distributors for Midnite Books next door. They're all Mafia, we're not that innocent—"

"Where will you get this elegant erotica?" I asked.

"Well, I'm a bit of an artist—"

Paula socked his shoulder hard. "You scum, Frank!"

"No, no, kidding, kidding. It's all Kitchell. I told him I'm not illustrating any porno."

I leaned back and watched Paula tickle his armpit. If Liam could have seen Paula like this, he might have liked her. I suddenly wished he'd walk in and see us and slide in familiarly next to me, but in my life I haven't expected things to be like that.

Just before school began, one evening when Liam was out, I got a call from Anthony. I had to sit down when I heard his voice because I found my feet tingling. "Did you really call me this summer?" he was asking me.

"Didn't Brother Nor tell you?"

"But I thought maybe you'd wanted just to talk to Brother Nor."

"No, I called to talk to you."

"He said you'd had a nice talk," said Anthony.

"I didn't know you were going to Oregon, Anthony. I wanted to read your new writing. How about it now?"

He said he would drop it by my classroom the first week of school. There was a crowd of new kids around my desk when he came. Liam's sister Malinda was in my class now. She wanted to make sure I knew she was Liam's sister and make sure her friends knew I knew who she was. And there were the kids with schedule conflicts and slips I had to sign. Anthony's head poked above the crowd, and he caught my eye. His arm snuck between two tenth graders and placed a small fat notebook, just like his last one, on my blotter. His hand looked bigger than the tenth-grade hands. It was dark, with beautiful veins and bony knuckles. It pulled back, and the crowd closed in around me. When the bell rang and everyone was gone, I had a moment of not being able to find the notebook under the papers that had descended, but then I touched its spiral binding and pulled it out. On the cover was written: Colloquy by Anthony Ognissanti. And it gave his address at the Saint Vincent Home and the year 1979.

Now that I was at school each day, I'd given Liam my extra key so he could come by and catch up on his sleep. He'd be there when I'd get home, and sometimes he'd have done the errands I'd asked him to do, and sometimes he'd still be asleep and I'd sneak upstairs and jump in with him. He never asked anything about school and didn't want me talking about it. I kept Anthony's new notebook in my backpack when I brought it home, and I looked at it only when Liam had gone out again after dark.

Now I could be sure that Anthony knew what he was doing. The Soliloquy might almost have been the work of an unself-conscious innocent, and I had worried that Anthony might soon lose whatever it was he seemed to have. But in the Colloquy it was clear he was drawing from a deep running source, which study and maturation couldn't choke off.

I sent him a note suggesting we meet once a week to discuss his work and the reading he was doing. I didn't care if my superiors found out. It was too important to me not to risk it. By asking him in writing I let him know it wasn't an idle offer. What I said was: "It's a discipline you need, Anthony, preparing your work for scrutiny, and I want to provide you with a serious reader (myself) to practice on."

He started coming by my classroom every Tuesday after his last class and after I'd finished with my middle-track tenth graders. One day on his way in he bumped into Malinda McGee on her way out, and I heard him ask where her brother was.

"Anthony, he's all fucked up," Malinda said. "Mom and Dad don't want him coming home even."

"Do you see him?" Anthony asked.

"He comes by at night, and they yell at each other, and he goes out. I hardly ever see him." That was all I could hear over the hall noise. He walked out with her but came back a minute later and closed the door carefully behind him.

The first Tuesday we'd gone over my criticisms in the margins of his notebook. The second we planned a reading list of books I thought he'd like. The third Tuesday I wanted to find out what he was discovering in the writing that he hadn't known when he started. It seemed to me, I told him, that unexpected discovery was the reward of creative work.

"But only the true things," Anthony added. "If I discover a thing that turns out not to be true when I think about it, I have to go back to where I went wrong and write fresh."

"If you could only do that in life—" I began, aware that my thought was the sort of obvious thing Anthony would never bother to say.

"But when you write about going wrong," he said, "it can still be true writing. I'd like it if only we could live like writing, where you can go wrong and still be right, if you can make it seem true."

"Sounds like a quibble, Anthony," I said, "a way to get around feeling guilty. Write it, make it true, and you're off the hook."

"That's why I like to write. I forget about being right or wrong." He smiled the smile I seldom saw. When it came it put a tingling in the back of my neck. Anthony was wearing a new blue shirt with snaps, which his sister must have bought him in Oregon, and no sweater yet because it was still September and warm and fresh. He was longer, his face fuller than in the spring, but he was still the permanent-looking Anthony, contained inside himself, calm, quiet, bony. He looked over the desk at me for five seconds with his smile, but I still see it when I want to because it was that important to me.

"And when you're not writing?" I asked.

"Well, I can be forgiven at least, if I'm wrong," he said and then added, "But when I'm writing it has nothing to do with forgiveness either. It has nothing to do with forgiveness or guilt." He leaned back in the creaky chair by my desk and gave a shrug, as if this phenomenon of the guiltlessness of truth was to be wondered at.

"I never feel guilt," I found myself saying. "It's a thought I don't have. I feel shame, perhaps, yes, I've felt shame—"

"Burt—" he began. I had gotten him used to calling me Burt. "Have you ever taken something from a friend?"

"Something?"

"Have you ever taken love from a friend?"

"My own love?"

"Your own love, someone else's love, both."

"Have I?" I wondered.

"There's a thing happening in me I can't stop," Anthony said. "The more I think I shouldn't let it, the more it happens."

What he was saying made me think of the Colloquy, where his characters, David and Jonathan he calls them, are considering the unlikelihood of their remaining friends when one, and you don't know which, is about to take away the other's girl. "And that seems to be your subject now, in your writing," I said.

"But you've been saying I shouldn't be sure how I want the story to end."

"Your characters might be teaching you something you don't know yet," I said, "and you should write to find it out."

"But what I know already is what's happening inside them, and that it's true what my Jonathan character is about to do in spite of himself."

I wished he hadn't told me it was going to be Jonathan because it spoiled my chance of judging the plot as it revealed itself, but I immediately saw I should have picked up more clues than I had. Talking with my other students, the best ones even, I always felt I knew more what they were doing than they did. It was a smug relaxation I fell into. But Anthony took that small pleasure away. My sense of teaching began to change when I discovered what it was to be engaged with someone who wanted my questions more than my answers. I was getting spoiled for teaching only average kids the rest of my life.

"But I was only saying you might not know everything you'll eventually know," I said.

"Of course," said Anthony, always ready to see what I meant.

I knew I could ask him about Nell now. It was no longer the way Liam had said it was when Anthony had wanted someone who didn't know him to help him, and maybe that had been only Liam's deviousness to keep an attachment from developing. On our fourth Tuesday, or so, I mentioned to Anthony that I was tutoring a friend of his on Saturday mornings.

"Nell," he said.

"Does she say anything about it?" I asked.

"She says her father pays for it, but it's supposed to be a secret."

I told him it was all right if I did tutoring, but it had to be separate from school.

"What about with me then?"

I said he was tutoring me as much as I was tutoring him, but he looked as if he didn't quite swallow that. "Your book was the best thing to get Nell to read," I said. "If you could hear her talking about you—"

"Of course, it's Nell I think I'm taking away from Ladro," he said.

"I thought."

"He's my best friend. We used to hate each other in eighth grade, but in ninth we got to be friends, when my parents died. We've been best friends all through high school."

"He's an unlikely best friend for you."

"This is what Ladro's like," Anthony began, sitting forward with his elbows on the edge of my desk. "He's a loud stubborn guy. You can't convince him of anything. He gets something in his head and that's it. He holds a grudge forever. I used to be scared of him. He liked making people scared. But what kind of kid is scary when he's alone? That occurred to me. I stopped being scared of him when my parents died. How could I be scared after something like that? He knew that. He started to like me. He was a friend who didn't want to help me. Everyone was wanting to help me, adopt me, take care of me. I mean, I'm grateful—where would a fourteen-year-old kid have been anyway—"

"David's your Ladro character then," I said.

"Sort of a shadow of him, maybe, not just Ladro, not real."

"But your characters do seem real now," I said, "not like the Soliloquy where it was just that voice watching everything."

"I didn't know where I was then," said Anthony, as if it was a matter of fact. "Going to see my sister made me change though."

I began to feel my jealousy again, that someone else could do things for Anthony I couldn't. I had felt it a little when he talked about Ladro, but I felt it even more when he talked about Elsa.

"My sister used to hate me," Anthony said. "When I was little she didn't like me that much, and when I got older and started bothering her, she hated me. And then she married Martin Keeney and left us, and the only time I saw her was a trip the next summer when she came back and fought with our parents. Then they died, and she got strange, but Martin took her to some doctor in Oregon, and she went for a while, and then she wrote me a letter. I started to write her. It got me started writing my Soliloquy, thinking about what I'd written her but wanting to write it another way, for me alone. I keep all her letters to me. They're long, full of old stories. They'd only be interesting to me. After all, she's my sister. Our letters didn't start friendly. There were bad things she wanted to tell me I'd done, things our parents did. I had things to tell her too. This summer it was something for me to go around with her, shopping, having her pick something out for me at a store, me washing her dishes after dinner."

I asked if in the Colloquy where Jonathan, as Anthony called his own shadow, talks about the cold windy beach, it's out there he's talking about.

"More of a dream," said Anthony. "What he feels is he's on a wide flat stretch of sand, and it's beautiful, but too cold. He wants to tell David how he's been alone, because he's afraid David will be alone soon now thanks to him."

"And so, Anthony," I said with a coaxing smile, "how is it between you and Ladro?"

His long brown hands were flat on my desktop. He was looking at them, and so was I, following the traces of veins. I didn't want to touch his hands the way I did want to touch Liam's, though Liam's hands were scratched and stubby, with chewed nails.

"Ladro and I don't talk about it," Anthony said.

"And so is it true what you're writing, Anthony, since you're so concerned with being true? Your David and Jonathan are voices talking, but if Ladro doesn't talk—"

"But it's inside him."

Here came the point I most wanted to teach him, by means of this question: "But if in life someone keeps himself so inside, isn't it false to imagine this shadow of him who's so thoughtful and feeling?"

His answer was also a question: "Why do you think people are only what they know of themselves, Burt, when they're also what they keep inside?"

"I'm just asking a question, Anthony."

Then he said, more excited, "I don't want David to come in and say—" He stopped and wrote quickly in the margin of a page: "Hey, Jonathan, you fucking asshole, getting any pussy lately, fuckhead?" He smiled up at me, a little embarrassed. "That's the sort of thing Ladro says, Burt. But I want to write like a dream, where everything comes out."

When I think of our Tuesday discussions, they always came to a point like that, where Anthony said what he wanted to do. I suppose that was the best part of my teaching. I let him clarify thoughts. He said he always wrote best Tuesday nights after we talked.

One day at school when I went into the men's room, there was Ladro himself when he should have been in class. "Hi, Mr. Stokes," he said.

"Hi, Mr. Brown. Don't you have a class?"

"Got a pass." He was spitting into a sink in heavy, loud splats.

"Feeling sick?"

"Let me tell you something, Mr. Stokes. Maybe you can tell him. My friend Og. If there's anything ever in his life, I'm going to take it. When he doesn't expect it, that's when I'm going to. I'm going to take away what he thinks he's got. What he never worries about anyone going to take because he thinks he's got it. That's what I'll take. You want to tell him that? You tell him. He'll forget it anyway in a year. But I'm never going to forget it. I don't forget things. He knows that too, but he'll forget anyway."

I was standing at the urinal while he talked, but I found myself unable to pee. I zipped up and washed my hands at the sink next to his. Ladro was still spitting, when anyone else would have run dry.

"You going to tell him?" he asked me.

"Do you want me to?"

He looked at my face in the mirror for a while. "No, don't tell him," he said.

"All right, I won't."

"But if you do anyway," he said, "I won't mind. I don't care about that fucking asshole."

"Do you want to come talk about it with me, Ladro?" I asked.

Now he was looking at his own face. I could see a tear coming, and I knew he wouldn't want me to see that. I looked away.

"That fuckhead is fucking Nell," he said, choking up. He turned around and kicked the door to one of the stalls, and it slammed. He went down the row kicking the doors. I watched him as I dried my hands on a paper towel. He started back up the row, one slam after another. Then he looked for something else to kick. There went the wastebasket, rolling around the floor spilling paper towels. He kicked it again, and it rolled back toward him, and he kicked it a third time. It lodged under one of the stall dividers.

"Will you tell him, Mr. Stokes?"

"Only if you want me to."

"I don't."

"Then I won't." He put his hand out to me, and we shook hands. "Why don't you pick up the towels and put the wastebasket back," I said, "and then come talk to me sometime after school. Mondays, Wednesdays I'm free."

I had to help him dislodge the wastebasket. He thanked me, and I said I'd see him some afternoon, but he didn't come by.

And now it was clear that Anthony and Nell were together. I'd see her waiting for him on the library steps on cool October afternoons. On Halloween, I'm sure it was the two of them at my door, with brown bags over their heads, poking each other and snorting, though they never admitted it. And he'd come by my house on Saturday mornings to pick her up after her tutoring sessions. They'd both have coffee with me in the kitchen before they left. Liam told me he'd never come by on Saturdays till Nell was gone. He didn't know Anthony came too until once they stayed past noon, having a good talk over coffee, and Liam let himself in with his key.

"What's that?" said Anthony.

I went toward the door, but since each room in the round house looks into the center hall, and there stood Liam in the sun from the skylight, still in his Friday night street-punk outfit, all I could do was say, "It's Liam McGee."

He leaned in the door frame to the kitchen. "Hi, Anthony," he said. "Hi," he said to Nell. "I came by to help Mr. Stokes with the wiring on the third floor," he said, a quick improvisation I was grateful for.

"How do you know wiring?" asked Anthony.

"What you think I'm doing since school?" Liam said. "I'm taking fucking night courses. Electronics."

"I didn't know," said Anthony. "Hey, I see Malinda around. She's getting up there. I still think of your sisters as little kids."

"I'm going up and get started," Liam said.

I was rinsing out cups at the sink. I heard Nell whisper to Anthony, "He looks so tired . . . circles under his eyes."

"We'd better get going so you can work," Anthony said. "I didn't know you had Liam working for you."

"He knows what he's doing," I said, nervously making no sense.

"I haven't seen him in a while. So he's doing okay?"

"He's responsible for half the work on this house," I said.

Nell said, "Wouldn't you love to live in a round house, Anthony? And we could always be fixing it up."

After they left I went upstairs, worried. Liam's leather jacket lay on the second-floor landing, his boots flopped in the doorway to my bedroom. His jeans and T-shirt led me up to his pale bottom on my bed. "Hello, Mr. Electrician," I said.

He let out a muffled sigh into the sheets, then said softly, "I had a horrible night. Please fuck me. I really want it."

Usually our sex was more playful. This time it felt serious, and he seemed in a dream. I was almost afraid of hurting him, even though he kept saying yes, and then he fell right asleep when we were finally through.

Sometimes on Saturday mornings, Nell and I put our work aside and just talked. She knew I knew what was happening with her and Anthony. She told me Ladro had said he was going to beat her up. "It's funny, Mr. Stokes, how I still love Ladro. Why don't I stop loving him? We been together so long, and we always talked about getting married. We had names for our kids. He couldn't hurt me, even if he says he's going to. Ladro thinks I'm better than him. Like he couldn't figure why I even liked him. Now he figures I never did. I don't want to tell him I still love him, even though I love Anthony, because he gets sadder when I say nice things."

"He's not friends with Anthony anymore," I said.

"Are you kidding!"

"Anthony has this way of losing friends," I said.

"That kid Liam McGee was a friend of Anthony's," Nell told me as if I didn't know. "But Mr. Stokes, I mean I know he's working for you, but that kid's weird."

"Nell, remember when we talked about how Ladro would bump into me someday and we'd laugh about him giving me a hard time? You kids don't have perspective on yourselves. Liam's just in the same mess you all are."

"You can't tell me he's not weird," Nell said, looking at me at a funny angle.

"Why not?"

"Mr. Stokes, you're too nice of a guy."

We went back to our work. We'd read all of the Soliloquy, and I had to resort to an anthology of stories next. The excitement had gone out of our sessions, now that they were regular and paid for and Anthony wasn't our author. We looked forward to his knock at eleven, to sitting at the kitchen table with coffee and muffins.

Once he brought snapshots of his trip across the country. I told him he'd come within a few miles of my hometown on his bus trip. He'd been closer to my parents than I'd been in a long time. And we saw Elsa herself. I easily recognized her. "I didn't get a good picture of Martin," he said. Nell wanted to know why they didn't have children yet. "Elsa can't have children, it turns out," he said.

I was looking at Elsa's face, seeing lines of maturity. The wind on the beach blew her black hair around. A figure in the distance, walking away, must have been Martin.

"She can't have them?" asked Nell, as if such a thing couldn't be.

"Not everyone in the world has babies," I told her.

"Someday I want a baby," Nell said.

"I'm saving a copy of my book for my first kid, remember, Burt? In case, anyway." Anthony's lips were shiny from the butter on the muffins. He said he'd name a girl Clara after his mother.

"And a son after your father?" I asked, hoping he'd talk about him a little.

"But Umberto's a funny name for a kid," he said.

"Hey, don't I get to choose names?" Nell reached over and poked him in the stomach.

Anthony put on a troublemaking face. "Who said anything about having a kid with each other?"

"Let me hope you're not having a kid with each other," I said, while Nell tried to tickle him. When he got laughing he didn't seem like the same Anthony, as if he couldn't stand to laugh. Gasps and hisses came out his teeth, and his legs and arms flailed around the stool he was sitting on when Nell grabbed at his stomach and armpits. Then he started to get her. She slid off her stool and ran around and got behind me. "Enough, enough," I said.

I put my arm on Nell's shoulder to calm her down. "Who said we've even had a dry run?" said Anthony, still troublemaking.

"Anthony!"

"All right, enough," I said, raising my hand. "I make a rule of never discussing their sex lives with my students." I still held on to Nell's tensing shoulders.

"I don't know when Anthony's serious or he's kidding," she said to me. "I knew when Ladro was."

"So go get Ladro back," Anthony said.

"I don't want Ladro back."

"Then here I am," he said, spreading his arms out.

She slipped under my arm and went back to sit on her stool.

"Put your arms down, asshole," she said. "Besides, I like Umberto. It's real Italian."

I went back to looking through the pictures. "Where's this, Anthony?"

"Inside Elsa's house. It's too dark, and it's too bright outside with the ocean right there. That's Martin in the shadow reading."

"And so what sort of marriage do they have?"

Anthony told us how Martin was quiet and let Elsa tell him what to do. He'd been nice to Anthony, had taken him for rides in his jeep. It was Martin who'd said Elsa couldn't have children. His sperm count was okay, he'd told Anthony. Nell found that a little graphic and told Anthony to shut up. I had to raise my hand again and silence his retort.

Then Anthony wanted to tell me about Elsa. "She's left the church," he said, as if he didn't want to believe it. "So's Martin. She said it isn't divine love she needs anymore. I keep writing her letters about it."

In Elsa's book, The Letters Of My Dead Brother, you hear a serious seventeen-year-old explaining to his sister what he means by divine love. As with his talk about guilt and forgiveness, it seems to me he was quibbling. As for divine love, he'd simply not had enough human love to know that it could mean the same thing. I have to say the letters don't interest me much. They are only the bones over which, in his fiction, a beautiful skin stretches. Elsa's book is his fleshless skeleton in the ground.

But this Kitchell does know how to sell it. The Spondee Press is now a big operation, and with Frank and Paula moved to Providence, I wasn't surprised that Kitchell latched on to Elsa's book and made the sort of thing of it the Innocenzos wouldn't have let him do at all. No mottled brown cover or abstract woodcuts—this is one of those paperbacks you find in stacks in the discount bookstore chains.

I don't know what happened to the letters Elsa wrote to Anthony. Did Brother Nor return them to her, with all Anthony's belongings, after he died? I trust she's not opportunistic enough to try to publish them next. If Elsa Ognissanti, or rather Keeney, finds her way into print on her own, I'll—(I like this word processor. When I think of something for a blank space like this,

I can insert it, and the seam will close. And when this disc is full of characters, it will be a final revised edition. If ever I print it out, I won't have to see what I went through getting it right, where I stopped and started.)

Anthony revised by the old methods. He didn't even type. Our Tuesday afternoons were mostly spent weaving through the knots of his revisions, in smaller and smaller letters between the lines of thick blue strokes. Paula had told him around Christmas that the Spondee wanted the Colloquy too. Frank was already making sketches, and Kitchell expected the manuscript as soon as possible.

"But let's not hurry," I told Anthony.

"I know," he said. "I wish I'd waited till I was surer of the Soliloquy."

"Someday you'll have a complete set of your work, Anthony, in final revised editions, a boxed set from the Spondee Press."

"It makes me nervous when you fantasize about me, Burt," he said quietly.

I felt a little odd. I didn't know why I had a stake in a fantasy like that, his complete works, and I still don't know.

"Burt," he said, looking at me as though he were for a moment older than I, "you live too much for other people, more even than Brother Nor, or Monsignor, more than anyone."

I said to him, "Anthony, if you knew what was inside me, you'd see it's not so much for other people as for myself—"

"So you're a little more complicated than Ladro," he said with a short laugh. "I'll write about you someday, so you'll understand."

"Ah yes, not only what I know of myself, eh, but like a dream, where everything comes out," I said, quoting him.

Is it Nell now who knows me best of anyone? I've never lived with anyone else. Or is it Liam for all our times together? But Liam doesn't have a view of other people. Anthony didn't have a chance to write about me, but even if he had, I'm sure I never gave him more than a hint of enough to go on.

How does Nell feel about me now? She's talking again. She calls to me, down the stairs, when I get home. She says what she'd like for dinner. She even will come down, some nights, and sit with me in the kitchen. We face each other on our stools over soup or stew. She wants to lean against me sometimes and pulls her stool around beside mine. And I've been joining her watching television on the bed in her room. I have a book on my lap, but I look up at the screen now and then, and she leans against me. "Burt," she said last night, "is it funny for you to think that you're my husband?"

"Is it funny for you to think that you're my wife?"

"I think I'm Antonia's mother," she said.

"We oughtn't to talk about Antonia. Last time we did, remember how it was?"

"I think I'm your wife then," she said, her hand squeezing my wrist. Then she giggled. "Mrs. Constantinidis doesn't think I am."

After her glimpses of Liam in states of undress, Mrs. Constantinidis wasn't pleased with another teenager, and a girl, and pregnant, moving in with me. The day Nell was collecting all her stuff from her parents', I'd shown Mrs. Constantinidis around the house. I was proudest of my job on the staircase, every spindle sanded and painted, broken ones replaced, the cracked bannister mended. I saw Mrs. Constantinidis widen her eyes as she walked through the arched door from the entryway to the skylit center hall. The black bannister curves up like a whip over the dining-room door to the landing, and the same graceful curve repeats above to the third floor.

Mrs. Constantinidis looked into each of the rooms, nodding and twiddling her fingers, and then slowly went up. She paused halfway and said, "The staircase is good, Mr. Stokes." On the second floor she looked into my bedroom and asked with narrowed eyes if this was where my bride would sleep too.

"Mrs. Constantinidis," I said, "you have to believe we're married. I'll show you the license."

"I don't want to see your license," she said. She walked around the landing, past what would be the baby's room to what I called the guest room with its new bed for Nell. "The things that go on here I don't even want to know. And will there be fewer comings and goings in this house now, Mr. Stokes? The man next door asks questions."

While she was looking at the bathroom, I felt I had to say, "I'm sorry, Mrs. Constantinidis, if I trouble you, but even if this is your house, I have a right to privacy, and I don't have to apologize for what you may think I do here."

"The bathroom is good," she said, "beautiful old tiles—"

She didn't want to struggle to the third floor, since it wasn't finished anyway, but she looked up at the new skylight and asked if I'd been out on the roof. I told her I'd redone it.

"I don't want to be sued when someone falls off my roof," she said.

"I've thought of putting a low railing, if I can find an old iron one. It's nice in summer up there."

"Absolutely no one on the roof," she said, heading downstairs. I followed silently. At the front door she told me she might want to have her agent look over the place sometime. It was the casual sort of threat she never followed up on, so I just nodded. "Your bride is lucky to be moving into a house like this, you know. This is the house I moved into as a bride." A week later we got a congratulatory card, bride and groom on a wedding cake, which I recognized from the rack at the all-night corner store, signed Hestia Constantinidis, with a check for five dollars enclosed.

There's no one else in my life, now that I see my parents so seldom, who causes me to feel such shame. I feel it really is her house, and I know the things I've done in it are even beyond what she imagines. Up to the time he left, Liam was even taking calls on my phone. He was on a list for out-of-town businessmen to call and arrange meetings in their hotel rooms. Twice when he was out, a confused, nervous voice wanted to know if I was Liam. I asked if it was Mr. McGee. "Who? No, no," the voice said and hung up.

Liam arrived later on Saturday afternoons now, to be sure not to run into Anthony again. One Saturday an expensive thirty-five-millimeter camera was hanging around his neck. "I borrowed it from someone," he said. "I thought maybe you could take some pictures."

"What for?"

"You know the kind of pictures I mean," he said, heading upstairs.

"What for?" I asked again.

"I could use them."

He was sitting on the edge of the bed by the time I came in. I stood in the door and looked across at him, not feeling good about his being there at all.

"What's the big fucking deal?" he said.

"I wouldn't know how to use that camera."

"You push the button," he said.

"Who's going to develop film of—"

"I know a place develops anything."

"Liam, you've been sort of down these days," I said.

"So?"

"When you came over that time Anthony was here, after that horrible night, remember, and you didn't tell me anything about it, and I don't know what's going on with you—"

"I was just fucked up that night."

I sat down beside him. He leaned forward, elbows on knees, and I rubbed his shoulders, our sign of comfort. I kept rubbing through his T-shirt, then put my hands up inside on his skin. "Why do you want to get into these things, Liam?"

"It's fun," he said.

"Is it fun?"

"How would you know, Burt? I like it. It's fun when it's going on. All the guys, and you don't know what's coming next. I don't give a fuck if I get fucked up some nights. There's times I really fucking take off, see what I mean? We been that way too. You really took off that time after I saw Anthony here."

"But I wasn't even sure you were here or where you were."

"I was here, and I was gone too," he said.

"But what do you want pictures for?"

"If I have pictures," he said, "then a guy I know can show them around to guys. To make some money, Burt, you know. And this guy says I can even make some more like just for pictures. And it'd be sort of fun taking them, you and me."

"Someone might recognize the house," I said.

"Yeah, sure. Don't be so fucked. Look, we can take them on the third floor in all the sun. There's just walls and windows— could be anywhere. There's a timer on the shutter—"

"You expect me to be in them?"

"Maybe just your hand, reaching, or your legs or something, so it could be anyone. Is the ladder up there? We could use it, me sort of hanging on it." He stood up, taking the camera from the bedside table, and said back to me, "Come on, Burt."

"It'll be cold up there with your clothes off," I said.

"Bring the blue quilt then, and a bottle of oil, and some kleenex. Come on, Burt." He was going up the stairs. "It's sunny, it's perfect for it."

He brought the pictures over when they were done. They somehow seemed like normal snapshots to me. He looked happy in them, innocent, playing with himself, just for fun. We did more the next Saturday, and then he put the camera on a windowsill and set the timer, and more of me got into some of the pictures. And that second time he brought tight pants and different kinds of underwear to put on and take off. Why didn't it embarrass me? I began to think I had a feeling for taking those pictures. I'd suggest he do this or do that, in different lights, and I'd take him from one angle or another.

He had two sets printed from that day and gave me one. I've never burnt the pictures, as I should do. I've put them in a pie-shaped wasted space in the dining room wall beside the built-in drawers, which I can get to only by pulling out the drawers and reaching in. I've kept them not to remind me how he looked, skinny, winter pale, slightly pimply, but what I felt like with him, I who have had so little of that. I didn't burn them when he left town the first time, and now that he's disappeared again, I still haven't.

He brought the camera a third time and said he wanted to make ones with more of me, just not showing my face. I had a different idea to try out. These sorts of pictures, I thought, are always taken as if by a third person, across the room, watching, never from the view of one of the two subjects. It seemed I could make the camera my eye during sex and preserve the angle of my glances down our bodies. But the light was wrong, or I didn't set things right, because nothing came out. Liam showed me the wasted blank negatives, and I reimbursed him for the developing, since it had been my idea. He didn't bring the camera again.

One night Liam said he wanted to take me to dinner at the

Serenata and he'd pay for everything. I told him he didn't have to do that.

"I'm sick of always being fucking paid for," he said.

We went late, so it wouldn't be crowded. He started off trying to make it different from the way it usually was between us, but I was slightly nervous, looking out for people I knew, and I wasn't acting the way he might have hoped I would.

"What cheesy decorations for a restaurant," he said, looking at the plastic logs flickering on the wall. "Of course, I go out sometimes to real class restaurants downtown."

"Have you seen your parents lately?" I asked. "Malinda says she never sees you."

"Malinda's a good kid. I like Malinda."

"Do you miss being at home with her?"

"I see her. I go home to change clothes. My closet's all I got at home. I come in the kitchen door, slip in, get what I need, and I'm fucking out of there."

"Don't your parents wonder how you're getting by?"

"See, Burt, what I tell them is I'm an electrician."

"You're going to night school to become an electrician was the story I heard."

"Yeah, but the way they heard it is I'm taking classes at night and I'm apprenticing in the day to this electrician and I'm renting a room—"

"Liam, if they swallow all that, why aren't they more proud of this hard-working son of theirs?"

"They don't swallow it. They just don't want to find out anything. They can't trust me. Did they ever trust me? Do your parents trust you? They probably always trusted you. My parents never fucking trusted me for anything. Why should they start trusting me? They come in that night of Anthony's fire, and slam comes my mom in the room and finds me teaching Anthony to put his little dick up my ass, and how do you think she trusts me! You know what she says after the funeral? You want to hear the worst thing I ever heard her say? She says, 'Well, I can only say it's good they're dead because if they ever found out what you were doing with their innocent boy, they'd die of disgust anyway.' She says that. That's my mom, with her church groups. How fucked up is she! You can see she didn't exactly like my idea about them adopting Anthony. 'We know what you want him for a little brother for. You're perverted.' That's my mom—she actually talks like that."

"Talk a little quieter," I said.

He lowered his voice. "Burt, what are you always worried for? You put up with me when you want a good fuck, but you don't want me around when your pal Paula might drop by and see your little slimy friend Liam all moved in."

"You go off in the evening," I said. "I didn't say you had to."

"Remember when you had the Innocenzos coming for dinner and I had to go?"

"That was last spring—that was just once."

"I never spent a fucking evening at the round house ever."

"You always went out—"

"I had to go make some bucks is what I had to do." Liam's face was tight and furious, his lips thin, his eyes squinting at me.

"There's a way around this," I said.

"What!" he said, suddenly loud again, and a few heads turned.

I said, "You can always spend tonight there."

He looked at the drying spaghetti sauce stuck on his plate. I drank my wine, which they hadn't served him because he wasn't old enough. "Sleep over?"

I nodded, though in a certain way I didn't want him to. I didn't want to get up from bed with him, early and cold, and get ready for school, leaving him there. Going to school, from him, would seem strange. Better that he just be there for a time every afternoon when I got home.

He reached into his leather jacket for his wallet and pulled out a twenty and held it in the air for the waitress to see. He smiled politely at her as she took the money, and he smiled again when she brought his change.

"Can I at least pay the tip?" I asked.

"Fuck no," said Liam.

We didn't have sex that night, just lay together and fell asleep, but neither of us could sleep long in any position together, so we turned apart, touching only my knee to his calf, and I slipped out in the morning without waking him. We didn't sleep together again.

It was odd having coffee with Paula in the faculty room that day. And she was pushing me about why I didn't spend more time with her and Frank and want to meet the friends they had for me to meet. "You're in danger of being surrounded with kids," she said. "You know what I get from Frank? He has nothing to do with kids. He doesn't even listen when I rattle on about school. It's a relief."

"Doesn't he want to have kids of his own?" I asked.

"Oh, that's another thing entirely," said Paula.

I did fly out to visit my parents for Christmas. It's the last time I've seen them. I had Liam keep an eye on the round house while I was gone, and I'm sure he brought people there, but I didn't want to know, as long as everything was the same when I got back, which it was.

That winter things stayed as they'd been. I didn't care as much about my teaching. Liam came and went, Anthony put his Colloquy in final form, Nell slogged along through the story anthology and wondered if we could read Anthony's new book next. I thought it would upset her because, as she seemed to know, it had something to do with her. "Why don't you think I can face things, Mr. Stokes?" she wanted to know.

One Tuesday in early spring, Anthony brought me a fair copy of the Colloquy for my last suggestions. I read it straight through that night, and he came in Wednesday, expecting me to want him to alter this or that, but I told him to leave it as it was.

"I don't feel relieved," he said. "I don't like to have finished something."

The door to my classroom swung open and banged against the wall. I couldn't see who was there, but I heard a voice that could have been Ladro's say, "Fuck!" When I got up to close the door, the boy had disappeared down the hall.

Anthony looked glum when I sat down at my desk again and asked him if he recognized the voice.

"I don't think it was," he said, knowing whom I meant.

"But I told him last fall to come talk some afternoon, and he never did. I'd hate to think he finally did and found you here."

"Talk about what?"

"What it is to have your best friend—"

"He wouldn't talk to you about that," Anthony said.

Frank was spending that afternoon at the library and was going to walk by the high school and pick up the manuscript for delivery to Kitchell. He met Anthony and me on the steps of the gym, and we walked across the parking lot to the bus stop in front of the town hall, where Frank would catch his bus downtown and I would descend one side of the hill, Anthony the other. We waited with Frank in a light rain, the Colloquy safe in his backpack. Frank is a mostly self-absorbed person, and when he tries to make conversation, questions pop out of him with no relation to anything that's been said. "Hey, Antonio, what part of Italy's your family from?" he asked at random.

"We're not even really Italian. We're Sammarinese. My grandmother's still alive there." Anthony had to explain to me that San Marino is a country of its own, surrounded by Italy but not part of it.

"I been there, Burt," said Frank. "You take a bus up from Rimini. It's a real tourist trap of a tiny country. It's mostly a huge rock with a town on the sides and three old fortresses along the top. We gave it a look on our northern Italy trip, our honeymoon. Verona, Venezia, Ravenna, Firenze—What's your grandma do there, Antonio, sell souvenirs? That's all anybody does there."

"She's too old for that. She's in a nursing home. She's never been over here, and I've never been there. So what part of Italy's your family from, Francesco?"

"I've always wanted to be a Florentine, but we're from Brindisi. A pit. Here's my bus."

Frank leaped on before an old woman who wanted to get off could get down the steps. He waved at us from a window, swinging his backpack off and knocking a lady he'd climbed over. He held the pack up to the window and gave it a proud pat, for the manuscript it now contained. "When you read those words next," I said to Anthony, "they'll be in print."

"Actually," he said, "I've a copy at the Home I'm going to go over tonight again. I always make copies in case of a fire."

"But, Anthony," I said, "it's on to the next book now."

"I've already started," he said.

I watched him walking off in his thick black sweater, a little tighter on him now, down the sidewalk along the town hall, and I couldn't imagine him when he was a boy darting through that basement flipping off all the lights with Liam close behind.

Paula hoped Kitchell could get the Colloquy out for Anthony's graduation, but the Spondee was hectically involved in its new ventures and nothing got done on time. Meeting us for dinner after one of his van runs up to New Hampshire, Frank told me, "I'm just not a salesman, Burt. Kitchell wants a salesman. And I miss being home with Paula, and in my studio, and going out with you guys, Burt. I've had it with this Iambus." The van itself was called the Iambus, a cleverness of Kitchell's, and the distributing cooperative was called Iambus too.

Just before graduation, Paula let me know that it would be her last. They'd decided to move to Providence. Frank was going to take over the Trochee, and Paula was going to take some time off and have a baby at last.

The senior class had voted me faculty speaker, and my speech preoccupied me when I wanted to think about Paula's move, and about Anthony. I couldn't dream up anything striking or original enough to be proud of. I scribbled some lines using my experience fixing up the round house as a metaphor for high school, with the ninth-grade basement up to the senior-year view from the third floor and graduation through the skylight into the larger world. But I had trouble with eleventh-grade bedrooms and realized I'd be more amusing than inspirational. What I decided to do instead was talk about my own high school, how different it had been. How could kids in a chain-link-fence town packed with triple-deckers, no parks, no yards, imagine my cornfield? I told them they'd likely not see the beauty of it. Gentle rolling land, a house and barns in a clump of trees, another house and barns on the horizon, no sea, no hills, no city. I didn't mean any implicit criticism of our own school administration and, if anything, went too far in saying that my high school wasn't real, was something that can't be, that it's only here in our town, now, this way, that we can face our hard modern lives, something like that, as though I, too, had grown up coming here. The speech came out shorter than I'd hoped, but they applauded longer than for the mayor when he spoke.

It was sweltering in the sun on top of the hill, not a breeze. It's the only place in our town that opens up, where you can see far, even in summer haze to the sea's edge. I milled about with everyone else long after the ceremony. Families picnicked on the lawn between the high school and the library. Anthony was there with Brother Nor. They joined Paula and Frank and me for a sandwich. We could only act as proud as Anthony allowed us to, but Paula and I, and clearly Brother Nor, felt very proud of him that day, the way his parents would have.

"Ladro made it," said Anthony aside to me.

"You didn't think he would?"

"Nell said one of his lines was how he was going to flunk his courses because she wasn't making him study anymore, and poor Nell was afraid he wouldn't."

Brother Nor, in slacks for his outing, sat beside me cross-legged and unwrapped the plastic from a tuna sandwich. "Mr. Stokes, your speech was quite to the point. These young people have little sense of that world there." He stretched his hand out to the skyscrapers downtown, to the harbor. "And they certainly have little sense of their teachers as people who went to high school too, who were difficult, who needed help."

"It was hard to come up with something," I said.

"Burt drove us crazy, desperate over that speech," said Paula.

"After all the compositions I've assigned them, it had to be good," I said.

"I liked best the part about someone looking after you out there," said Anthony. "That's something that's the same everywhere, I guess. I would've thought out there people wouldn't feel part of a town as much and care about each other. When I rode through on the bus, it seemed empty there. When do you see people? Not that they'd be unfriendly, but when do you see each other? Like the beach where Elsa lived, so empty—"

"Anthony's empty beach again," said Brother Nor. It seemed Anthony had shown him bits of the Colloquy, but this time I knew he couldn't possibly see it as devotional writing, couldn't possibly.

"I've drawn that beach," said Frank. "I've done a bunch of pen-and-inks this time. The beach, the windswept heights—they've got a biblical feeling, I hope. Lone small figures, David and Jonathan—"

"But you don't show faces, Francesco."

"No faces, Antonio mio, I promise, everything's in shadow."

"Can we count on copies this summer?" asked Brother Nor.

"I'll bring them by as I did before," I said.

"But you know that Anthony won't be with us now," Brother Nor said. "He'll have his own place."

Anthony never told me his news. I'd imagined he'd go on living at the Saint Vincent Home, even after he started college, since it's a commuter school downtown. My only fear had been that he'd go out to visit Elsa again for the summer.

"I got a room in a rooming house down the hill, down past the church," Anthony said. "It's Martin who sent the money. He's making enough in computers out there. It's for my graduation, a summer living on my own, just to write."

"Great news!" said Paula, lifting her glass of ginger ale in lieu of beer.

"You see what a reconciliation there's been," said Brother Nor to me. "It's not just Martin Keeney, of course, it's Elsa. She's written me as well. She wants her brother to have this time for himself before he has to get a night job in the fall and go to classes."

Paula said, "It's the storyteller in Anthony that springs news like this when we don't expect it."

"The way he had me fooled all the way through his book," said Brother Nor. "Of course, I was thinking of David's subsequent behavior with Bathsheba, but it never occurred to me it was the serious Jonathan who was finding himself so torn."

"You've read the whole book?" I asked.

"This time Anthony wasn't so shy. He let me see what he'd written before he gave it to print. Not that I'd presume to change a word—"

"It's Anthony's fine sense of what to select," said Frank, taking the conversation over in his enthusiastic way. "It's like a drawing or anything else. There's everything in the world you can show.

But something comes to you, an inspiration. You choose just those single few things, and you get them right. The clues, the hints all add up to the one right thing."

I had not been one to believe in inspiration. I used to feel I could help my students make progress, from one point, wherever it might have been, to the next, but inspiration, I find, is beyond such points, not a continuum but a leap. There was Anthony, knowing enough all at once, and calm about it, hard-working, modest.

"But it's not a mystery story," said Paula. "It's not as important who's taking love from whom, as that love is there to take and be taken."

I wanted to add something to this serious discussion, but all I could think of was to ask, "And what does the author think?"

Anthony stopped midway in his tuna sandwich and held it before him. He was lying on his side, chin on his other hand, elbow in the grass. He took another bite and thought some more. "What I think I wrote best was the ending, when Jonathan isn't able to stop himself talking, and David only listens. And David's face gets colder and colder until it doesn't move. You know then what's happened." He went back to his sandwich.

"It is a mystery story in its way," said Brother Nor, "but the story of a greater mystery, of course." Paula conceded him a smile. He went on to say that they were having a farewell dinner for Anthony that night at the Home and he feared they had to be on their way soon to make preparations.

Other former students of mine kept coming up and telling me how they'd liked my speech and introducing me to their parents. Not far away I saw Ladro and his parents and brothers and sisters. I wanted to go present myself to them, but I was stalled along the way. Nell, who had been on a refreshment committee, squeezed by me in the crowd on her way, finally, to congratulate Anthony. I tried to catch sight of her being introduced to Brother Nor. What sort of moment was that for Anthony?

In the midst of the crowd I found myself being congratulatory to a succession of students, making smiley conversation with parents, and even talking shop with the tedious coordinator of the English curriculum. I wrote off the rest of the afternoon to duty.

The next week, after the final faculty meeting, I faced another summer of working on the house, and helping Paula and Frank get ready for their move, and, I hoped, seeing something of Anthony, now he was on his own.

"I can't stand it in town here another summer," said Liam one afternoon on the roof. "Don't you ever want to go to the beach and get out of here?"

"I've never been a beach person," I said.

"I could live on a beach. I'm sick of working on this fucking house. Don't be surprised, Burt, someday when I don't show up."

Liam had been talking like that long enough for me not to take note of it anymore. He'd positioned himself behind the chimney so that even if people were looking out the windows of the condominiums in the former schoolhouse they couldn't see that he was lying naked on the towel. "I want to get my butt as brown as the rest of me this summer," he said. "I want to go to some faraway beach."

I just drank my beer and read.

I can't figure out how to connect this. The word processor can transplant it later on, but I have to write it here now. We were watching television together last night, Nell and I, and she was leaning against me and I thought she was watching the program too. Then I thought she'd fallen asleep. Then I just barely saw her eyes were open and she was staring along my body, and her fingers were on one of the buttons of my shirt. I looked up, pretending to watch the television, but I could only think of her lying there alongside me, head on my shoulder.

"Burt, do you love me?" she said in a whisper.

"Yes, I do," I said.

"Are you my husband?"

"As long as you want me to be."

"What are we going to do next?" she asked.

"What do you mean, Nell?"

"Shouldn't a husband and wife make love to each other?" she asked.

"But after having the baby—"

"I think I'm ready for it now. I think I want to. Would you want to, Burt?"

"I haven't done anything like that, with anyone, since Liam last summer," I said.

"And I haven't since I got pregnant," she said, "almost as long ago."

"It's funny how we know all these things about each other," I said.

"Since you liked doing it with Liam, would you like doing it with me?"

"It would be different, Nell. I didn't feel I loved Liam."

"But I'm not wild like him."

"I don't want to be wild."

"Remember when I used to think Liam was weird?" she said. "I don't think he was weird. If anyone's weird, it's me. Why do I want you to make love with me, Burt?"

"Do you love me?" I asked.

"I must love you. But it's not like Anthony. It's not like Ladro."

I said we both had things to discover.

"But how would we even start?" Nell asked.

I hugged her tighter. "I don't know."

"You're handsome, Burt," she said, still looking down along my body.

I put my hand on her cheek. "Nell—" She squeezed me. "I could come in here tonight to sleep," I said, "and we'd see—"

"No, I want to come in to you, to the big bed, where Mr. and Mrs. Stokes should sleep."

Without saying more, we turned off the television and went into the other bedroom. I didn't feel nervous, and she didn't seem to. We were in the dark. Soon I was feeling her naked in my bed and she had hold of me. It was the safe time of the month for her, she said.

At moments I felt she was Liam, and then I knew she was Nell. I was in a dark dream, tumbling, surging. Did she think I was Anthony? I even pretended I was Anthony, at first, to get myself going, even for a moment that I was Anthony with Liam. But I came back to Nell and me. In the midst of it I saw Anthony come running to me, over a hill, barefoot, all in tears, saying

Nell's pregnant and she wants an abortion. And here was my Nell beneath me. And I thought that now I'd been inside Liam, and inside Nell, in the two most secret places Anthony had been in his life.

Obloquy

Nell should have graduated today. They are all up the hill picnicking inside the gym because it's raining. Faye wondered if I'd go to lunch with her, but I told her I had to catch up on the word processor.

Nell's aunt called me again this morning. I could hardly talk to her with Faye one desk away. She had last called just after Antonia was born, and now she said, "I'm calling, Mr. Stokes, to see how the baby is, and how is Nell."

I held the receiver close, my hand over it, and turned my back to Faye across the aisle. "We made a decision," I said. I waited, not knowing what to say, and she waited for me to speak. Suddenly Faye started typing at her furious speed, and I was able to say into the receiver, "We've given Antonia up for adoption." I heard a gasp, then she hung up the phone. I don't know if Nell will think I did the right thing.

Nell has not been any happier lately, but she has been calmer. Now I kiss her when I come home, and sometimes we sit side by side on the living room couch, our arms around each other, as if we were a young couple in love. We have slept together a few times more, but not every night, and when we do, I manage to fall asleep, even if Nell is leaning against me. She isn't squirmy the way Liam was.

She's been talking about how she loved Anthony. A few days ago we were on the couch, with iced tea to cool us off. It was too hot out to cook a meal. She put one thin arm gently over my shoulders, and her fingers fiddled with the strap on my overalls.

"You know what we used to do, Anthony and me? We met after school at the library, in the O's. He said that's where he'll end up someday, on the O shelves. Anyway, we used to put our chairs close and lean up to the table and hold hands and touch each other's legs under the table. It was worse than making out at the movies with Ladro. We had to keep it quiet. Anyone could walk by. We didn't really do anything. It was so exciting, Burt, just that way."

"With Liam too," I said, "it was better thinking about it beforehand, leading up to—"

"I have to tell you something I know about Liam," Nell said. "I didn't want to tell you after Anthony died. He got Anthony to do it with him when they were kids."

"Anthony told you?"

"He told me he'd never want to do it again, but he was glad he did it, to see what it was like. Anthony was funny, Burt. He got all excited about sex. He wasn't one of those guilty ones like Ladro. Is the tea okay?" I said it was. "I'm going to start helping more," said Nell. "I could make some tuna salad for dinner."

"You don't have to, unless you want to."

"Burt, you were one of those guilty ones when you were in school, I bet."

"I didn't do anything till college."

"But then."

"It wasn't that I was guilty," I said.

"But now your parents don't even know you're married," said Nell. "You could tell them now. You don't have to say about Antonia. You could say you and me'd just got married."

"I still want to wait, Nell, a little longer." I felt bad saying it, but I think Nell may begin to want to go back to her old life, and why should I put my parents through news of divorce right after news of marriage? I changed the subject back. "You made it sound, Nell, as if what he did with Liam wasn't so upsetting to Anthony."

"You knew about it too?"

"Liam had to tell me, of course, and that Anthony told him never to tell anyone. He said Anthony stopped being friends with him then."

"Anthony thought Liam was so weird, Burt. He said Liam acted like there was always something wrong, people didn't like him. Anthony told me he'd be friends with him still, only he didn't know what they could do together. You didn't go riding bikes anymore and thinking you're being bad to stay up late watching TV."

"But they had a fight at the end," I said. "I saw it, across the parking lot. They went off in different directions, but I walked over and saw drops of blood on the gym steps."

"Anthony told me he had to bite like a dog and scratch him," Nell said. "They were hanging around after school, and Liam kept grabbing at him and trying to wrestle. Anthony said Liam grabbed at him again coming out of the gym. He was asking for it. Anthony couldn't stand it. He fought back, and Liam got him in some hold, and Anthony had to bite him, and he was scratching and telling Liam to get off him. Anthony really bit him, Burt. It broke the skin."

"Still, a year later he wanted me to give Liam a copy of the Soliloquy."

"You don't know how Anthony was, Burt. Liam was still in his life, important, you know, even when he never saw him again."

"But then he didn't give him the Colloquy."

"The Colloquy he sent to Ladro," Nell said. "He sent it to him at his job. It's good Ladro wouldn't ever read it."

Later that evening, when we were having Nell's tuna salad in the kitchen, she asked me, "Why do you think Anthony loved me, Burt?"

I hadn't ever considered the question as such. Nell didn't start to look beautiful until the second time you saw her, and she looked more beautiful the third. She was skinny and pale, like Liam, but tougher in her fine-boned way, and matter-of-fact.

Anthony could kid her around, and she'd hold up. I could see he liked that. It must also have been his excitement over the possibility of sex. And then she was going with Ladro—that was something too. What I said to Nell was, "How could he not love you, Nell?"

"My parents don't much," she said.

"They do, but they don't know how."

"Who knows how?"

I thought of saying I didn't know myself, but I would try, but while I was thinking, she started talking about Anthony.

"It was so good the times we got to be in bed, Anthony and me. My parents didn't know I was going afternoons to his rooming house. I said I was at Ruthie's or Josie's. After those times under the table in the O's, it was something coming to his actual room. I'd get in downstairs sticking my library card in the door and flipping the lock. I'd sneak up to his room without him hearing. He'd be writing at his table by the window. Once I said real loud suddenly, 'How come your books all end in quy?' and he jumped. He wouldn't tell me. He made me look up in the dictionary what obloquy meant. Usually I'd sneak in and tickle him. We'd be on the little shaky bed pretty soon. He had his package of safes ready. Do you mind me talking about it, Burt?" I shook my head. "You know what Anthony liked most?" Her elbows were on the table on either side of her plate of tuna salad, which she was only picking at.

"What?" I said.

"Staying inside me afterwards, and falling asleep like that, him and me."

I felt tingly hearing that, but I said, "That's dangerous to do with a condom on."

"It never slipped off. That isn't how I got pregnant."

"I know," I said. "Anthony told me how it happened."

It didn't embarrass her. She said, "You thought Anthony was beautiful too, didn't you, Burt? You understand how I felt with him. I couldn't actually believe I was with him, like I didn't deserve him, like the way Ladro felt with me, or how Liam felt with you."

"Liam?"

"I mean, you were Liam's best teacher, everybody's best teacher, and Liam was with you all that time. I bet he couldn't actually believe he was with you."

I had only been thinking of Liam as furious with me.

That night, with Nell sleeping beside me, I had half-awake dreams, pictures of Liam and Anthony, on bikes, pedaling over the hill, racing, chasing each other. The hill means something in my dreams, the hill that separated us. The first night sleeping with Nell, a week ago, I had that glimpse of Anthony running to me over a hill, barefoot and in tears, but last summer, when he came to tell me about Nell being pregnant, he wasn't barefoot, he hadn't run. It was on a hot night in late August. I hoped it might be Liam at the door, since he'd been gone for weeks and I'd been finding myself missing him, worrying where he was, wondering if I'd been as tired of him as I'd thought. I'd begun to wish I'd asked him to spend another night. I might've gotten used to him there, I thought, despite his squirming sleep. The knock echoed in the empty round house as I came down the stairs. I pictured Liam on the other side of the door, prepared myself for him to act as if he was just dropping by for a minute, and I knew how I wanted him to stay.

But it was Anthony there, under the dim light, and I saw tears on his cheeks. He said right away, embarrassed and shaky, "I rang the bell and stood here waiting for you and started to cry. It's good to come to you, Burt. I couldn't go to Brother Nor. I couldn't go to Monsignor."

"What happened, Anthony?" The only other time I'd seen him uncalm was when Nell had tickled him in my kitchen. He came in, wiping his cheeks, and when I offered him iced tea he asked if he could have a beer instead. Sitting at the table, he got his news out in a backward way, his lips trembling. "I don't want Nell to have an abortion, Burt. She can't. She can't."

I must have begun to tremble too. When news comes, and you've been in your own worries, and then you're jolted like that, especially by an Anthony who means so much—I didn't know what to say and couldn't speak.

"Burt, we got pregnant. It was my laziness, taking a risk, being crazy. I thought I had a package of skins, but we'd used it up.

The drugstore was closed. Nell said I could try the all-night store, not yours, but there's one down near me, just a couple of blocks, it might have them, but there was a used skin from the day before, so why should I go out and interrupt what we were doing. See how stupid? It was way after we'd finished I saw it'd broke. We kept hoping we'd been lucky, but now we know we haven't been. She wants an abortion. She doesn't want to get married now."

All I could do was reach across the table and touch his shaky hand. His tears came again, and he wiped them with the hand I wasn't touching. Finally I could say, "I don't know what to do."

"She's Catholic too," he said with a gulp. "In her family, though, it doesn't mean anything to them." He sounded angry at everybody, himself too. He was drinking his beer down fast.

"If you knew the number of kids in this town who—" I began, thinking it wasn't what I should say, but it was easier to go back to being his teacher. I drew my hand to my side of the table.

"This was my perfect summer," Anthony said.

"You're lucky for that," I said, as firmly as I could, "but now you have to decide what to do."

"I couldn't go to Brother Nor."

I watched Anthony across the table, couldn't go around to him. His face was in his hands. When he looked up, I was looking at him. I said we could take our beers to the living room where it was cooler and comfortable. He followed me across the hall. I sat in my big chair, and he first sat on the rocker, looking dazed, and then after a few minutes stretched out on the couch, his head propped on the arm. It's an ugly overstuffed brown couch, missing a leg, its back corners leaning against the wall, and in the curved wall between is a window, open that night to what summer breeze there was. Anthony seemed long and flattened on the couch, bent up at the neck and at the skinny knees to fit. His jeans and shirt, his Western one with snaps, were baggy, as though there wasn't much of him underneath.

Lying there, staring at the ceiling, at the moldings Liam had scraped and sanded and painted with me, Anthony said, "I got off to a bad start with sex, Burt. I don't have to tell about it. It was just bad. It was the night my parents died. I didn't ever want to do it with anyone again. I wanted it to be a lonely thing. I did it just alone and thought how I was always on the other side of something, like the moths on my screen, and I could never get in, never get in. Then I listened to Ladro talking about him and Nell, and how it was when they were together. He always talked about getting pussy, so I used to think he and Nell did that, but they only got pretty heavy and close to it. Still, he understood it, as something you do with someone. To him it wasn't lonely—it was all going toward Nell. I'm not such a good Catholic as Ladro. I couldn't keep it down once I got with Nell myself. Then it seemed pointless to have been alone. The only thing I wanted was to be with her. Why hadn't I learned it earlier?"

"But how could you have learned it?" I asked. "There are people who never learn it. It takes time to learn."

"I'd better go to the bathroom," Anthony said. He found his way upstairs where he'd never been before, and I brought two fresh beers into the living room and waited for him. He came in and sat on the rocker instead of the couch. "You live in such a big house all alone, Burt," he said, a bit slurry from beer, which he wasn't used to. "I don't understand your being alone, when you could have somebody, you more than anyone."

"It's cheaper living here than in an apartment," I said.

"Nell and I would live in a house like this if we ever could," Anthony said. "It's just the way we'd want it. I'd do my writing on the third floor in the sun. Nell would bring up the baby, Clara, or if it's an Umberto, either Umberto or some better name. There'd be rooftops below, treetops, the distance. The baby could lie in the sun. I'd go and hug Nell, sitting on the floor next to our—" He started to break in tears again. The chair kept rocking, and he couldn't say anything more. Talking that way, he was doing it to himself.

I kept saying, "Oh, Anthony." That was all.

He got his voice for a minute and said in a quick gasp, "Or even in my little room in the rooming house, the three of us—"

"It could be that way," I said. He was crying quietly to himself, trying to hold it in. Then I said, "You have to think of Nell, too."

His eyes got darker, and he stood up from the chair and started walking to the couch, then to the door, from the door to the far

window and back to the chair. He was squeezing his hands and
with each swallow he gulped down tears, but he didn't wipe his
eyes, his cheeks. "No," he began to say, "no, she—" And then he
had to bite his lip to keep it still and swallow some more. His
walking helped him talk.

I kept saying Anthony to him in different ways, sad, worried,
comforting. I didn't know what to say.

"Nell, after what she taught me—" he began. "Nell—" He
looked at me, not believing it was Nell he was talking about.

"Does she know how hard it is for you to think of an—" I
wanted to say abortion.

"I tell her everything. She knows everything. She's smart, Burt.
Because she doesn't read doesn't mean she's not smart. I can
write, I can read, in ways I'm smart, but I'm not good at being
together with someone. I don't keep friends, you notice? Where's
Liam? And Ladro? Where's even Martin? After he took me
jeep-riding and sent all this money, what do I do for him? Elsa's
friends again, not friends actually, but we can be together and not
fight if it's for a short time, with Martin getting me out of the
house a lot. But I wouldn't move there. I get attached to one
person at a time. Now it's Nell. She knows what she wants—
finish school, work awhile, wait till I finish college to get married,
find a place, and when I'm teaching or whatever I do, then have a
kid, probably another, she'll stop work, but then she'll go back
later. She knows all that. That's why I love her. She isn't scared. I
was scared of my father. I was scared when I was little of riding
bikes with Liam. I was always scared of him, for a long time, and
I was scared of Ladro, even more last year when I was taking
Nell away. And I was scared of Brother Nor, and totally scared of
Monsignor, still. And my mother used to make me so scared with
the worst stories from the hospital. She used to tell me what she'd
seen, accident victims, every detail. She was always sad. I was
always scared I'd make her sadder."

"But there were scary things you did yourself, Liam told me,
the town hall basement—"

"I did do things to get scared. I used to snatch things, hide
things, make trouble, to make myself scared. Liam did the dangerous things, riding his bike without hands through intersections

without looking or climbing out high windows. I wasn't daring when I was little. I was just a troublemaker. My father would've killed me. I'd do anything secret and wrong. Do you know how scared I was about sex alone at the Home? How scared I was in the library when I used to feel under the table with Nell?"

"But now, in your own little room with her?"

"Buying skins the first time, how scared I was? But then in the room—she was more important than anything. Do you know what she did for me? There was so much I didn't have then. You think I was just your best student who brought you his brilliant writing and went back to his orphanage and wrote and wrote. And Ladro thought I was a good sort of friend to have, the sort other kids didn't know what to make of."

"But you weren't scared of him after your parents died, you said."

Anthony had stopped walking at the far window and was looking out, his back half turned to me. "I was still scared," he said, "but I didn't care what happened, that's what it was, if I got beat up, or had no friends, or if no one ever loved me. I didn't care about a thing. You can see why Ladro liked someone like that for a friend."

"And then Nell—"

"But first you, too, Burt. You, then Nell. Everything changed."

"And Paula too," I said right away, to cover my feelings.

"But it was changing before I had Paula," Anthony said. "It was you, and then later it was Nell. You showed me what I had in myself."

"Not at all," I said. "You brought it out on your own. You gave it to me one day at school, your work, and I took it home with me."

"No," Anthony said, "but before that, it was already you."

"But I hadn't talked to you before."

"But you talked to the class, and you talked one day about what words were for. You looked at me on the side of the room. You probably looked at everyone, but a couple of times I saw you looking at me, as if you saw what I had inside me."

"Brother Nor saw what you had inside you too."

"Brother Nor heard me crying in bed at night. He heard me in

screaming nightmares. He told me he'd never come in my room
if I had the latch on. He knew I had to be private, not like some
boys. He saw my sufferings. You saw everything I had that was
strong."

"So did Nell," I said.

Anthony had his hands on the window frame and was pressing
his cheek to the glass. I saw how he was trembling again, and
maybe tears were running even on the windowpane. I could go
over to him, do the comforting thing of putting an arm around
his shoulder.

"But Nell was later," he said. "And why are you so lonely,
Burt? Why can't someone do it for you?"

"Show me what I have that's strong? Well, you've done that
for me yourself," I said from across the room in my chair.

"I've never done—" he began, then he couldn't speak. Then he
said, "Nell loves you, too," in the backward way he had of saying
things.

"I love both of you," I said, not looking at him by the far
window but along the wall curving toward him.

"Burt, you could talk to her, let her talk to you about it. If you
could make her feel it was all right to have the baby—"

"I can talk to her," I said, "but I can't make her feel it's all
right, or it's not all right."

"You can talk to her."

"I can talk to her."

He crossed the room, leaned over me, and put his hands on my
shoulders and his cheek for a second against mine. I felt the tips
of my fingers reach up and touch his back on the blue Western
shirt his sister had bought him. Then he went back to the couch,
sat sideways stretching his legs out, and picked up the second
beer, which he hadn't touched yet. I felt my sweat all over,
seeping into my clothes, behind my knees, in the small of my
back.

"Is it cooling off outside?" I asked.

He reached his hand over the back of the couch and shook his
head as he touched the air in the window.

The next day I got out my Xerox of his summer work, the
Obloquy, and went through it again looking for things I hadn't

seen before. He had written it very fast, all excited, working every day in his little room, stacks of notes and sketches and false starts, winnowed down and neatly transcribed into another of his small notebooks. Frank, who was now happily managing the Trochee, had started a magazine of his own in Providence and wanted bits of the Obloquy for it. Anthony and I picked three likely fragments and sent them down, and Frank wrote back a Frank-ish letter:

Dear Burt, Antonio mio caro,

Everything's a mess. I'm no businessman. Paula's keeping the books, thank God. I mean the finances (books) not LITERATURE (books!)—that's _my_ job. Have you seen Kitchell's latest? Frankly I have my doubts. Now, see, I wouldn't give him your Obloquy, Anthony. The bits you sent are GREAT! Gets the Trochaic Review off on the right foot (so to speak). Not that I want to protect you from Kitch, though I think you're gonna need it, the bastard is climbing up that ol' ladder, but I want you all to myself! Every asshole thinks he can do this sort of thing. What does Kitchell have I don't? The point is, Paula and I are making the store a cozy little place where people come and hang out and don't feel they have to buy anything. Counting on Rare Books to carry us along. I'm becoming an expert (seriously). The other thing, definitely, of course, is we're whanging away at trying to get pregnant. No luck so far, but that never stopped me! You should see how happy Paula is not working. When are you (both of you, now that you're a big boy, Antonio) coming down to Prov to see us? After the 1st issue is out there'll be a party. We REQUIRE our authors' attendance. Black tie! In any case, I'm doing etchings for Obloquy. Real etchings (limited ed.) that we can reproduce offset for the Review. It'd be something if we get it together enough to do some Trochee BOOKS next year. That's why I don't want you going to that scum Kitchell. He's not speaking these days anyway, threatens to drop me from Iambus Distributing. Fuck him royally. Enclosed xeroxes of sketchings for etchings. Whaddaya think? Anthony, where do you get the way your mind works? I want to see how the whole thing fits when you're done. Leave it to Anthony, eh Burt, to make himself the king of his own little country. Must be the Sammarinese in him. I can't put into words (Plea of Inarticulation) what I think about the bits you sent. I shall let my sketches speak for themselves. Paula says to say again you have to come see us! Take the bus—Trochee's right down the block from bus station. LOVE, Francesco I (Paula too)

The writing got smaller at the bottom of the page, and the last words twisted up the right margin.

Frank's new sketches weren't like the Soliloquy's swirly frontispiece or the spare pen-and-inks for the Colloquy. They were minutely detailed: crumbling battlements with phone lines attached, shadowy cliffsides, a distant airplane in tumbling clouds. Frank draws beautifully. There was a portrait, at some distance, of King Og IX as a boy, in a castle window, looking enough like Anthony and enough not like him, but the digital watch on his wrist was distinctly the one the boys at the Home had given Anthony for graduation. And there was the huge marble tomb of King Umberto in a grove of whorly thick tree trunks with a slight figure kneeling, his back to us and a hole in the elbow of his sweater. And the coronation, a sort of medieval costume party in what I didn't yet recognize as Saint Vincent's Church, a tall bishop holding over their heads the crowns of the young king and queen, glimpsed through furls of pennants and robes. I'd think of Frank as a self-centered blowhard, and then he'd do a drawing that showed he understood Anthony as well as I thought I did.

Anthony and I had met quite regularly all summer to go over his work, at the library, or at the sub shop across from the high school, and I did see his room once. Liam hadn't shown up for a few days, and I'd begun to worry that he'd left town. I stopped by Anthony's with the excuse that I was in the neighborhood. The tall aluminum-sided Victorian house, with rotting porches and eaves, was sandwiched between the usual three-deckers. When I rang, a large sheepdog bounded to the door and clattered its toenails on the panes. Another roomer let me in, a young woman clutching her struggling cat out of reach of the dog. She pointed me upstairs. I felt uncertain just dropping by, but there was no way to have phoned him. I went to the door with a travel poster for San Marino taped to it, a castle on a rock, and knocked. I heard a chair scrape the floor, and there was Anthony, surprised, opening the door.

"It's certainly small," I said. The room was long enough for a cot and wide enough for a rickety table under the one window.

"I would've thought to invite you sometime," he said, "but it's not much of a place."

When he closed the door behind us, I felt closed in and oddly awkward with him. I looked at the stacks of paper on his table.

"Miss Burnham downstairs gives me used paper from her office," he said. "I use the back sides for first drafts."

There were library books stacked on the floor and on the bed, Kafka and Gide, I noticed, and Dinesen, from the latest installment of my reading list.

"Listen to this, Burt," he said, picking up a bilingual edition of The Poems of André Walter, by Gide. "It's the line I couldn't remember yesterday that I wanted to tell you: 'I think we live in someone else's dream and that's why we're so submissive.' See what I meant? I taped it up here in French by my desk."

On an index card, Anthony had written the lines:

Je crois que nous vivons dans le rêve d'un autre
Et que c'est pour cela que nous sommes si soumis.

That card is the only relic I still have of him. Brother Nor mailed it to me after Anthony died, and I keep it in my wallet.

"We could climb out on the porch roof," Anthony said. "I usually take my pillow out and read once it's shady."

He went to get some ice from the communal fridge downstairs, and I heard the dog snuffling at him in a friendly way. He brought up instant iced tea, and we climbed out the window and leaned against the aluminum siding, warm from the sun that had just passed the eave. I asked Anthony what he was doing writing an Obloquy when he had been in such good spirits all summer. "They go into the story, all my bad thoughts," he said, "so I'm bound to be happy the rest of the time."

"Is it writing about your father that does it?"

"You always think I'm writing about someone," said Anthony. "It's bad thoughts, not people."

"You do call him Umberto," I said.

"Because of Umberland, my country, and its tyrant king, Umberto," Anthony said, as if it was all real. "It's meant to be a cold island in the sea, with craggy mountains, the Land of Shadows. I love word origins, Burt, where it tells you in the dictionary, you know, what a word comes from—"

We spent the afternoon talking about what he was reading. It took a lot of my evenings to reread the books I'd recommended and keep ahead of Anthony, find questions to ask him.

When it neared four, and I imagined Nell might be coming, I said I had to go. When I left the house I relaxed again. Being with Anthony in his little room, even on that narrow balcony in the shade, had felt cramped. It hadn't been like having him come by my empty classroom or drop by the sunny airy round house, or meeting him at the library or the busy sub shop. I had never been alone in a small place with Anthony. It didn't seem to bother him the way it did me.

Later that week he got a letter, in Italian, telling him his grandmother had died. He could tell what it meant, but he said he took it to Brother Nor to be sure of every word. "Her name was Elsa Ognissanti like my sister," he told me. "She was eighty. She died in her sleep. It was this home for the elderly where she lived in San Marino. There will be a little money for Elsa and me, just a little." It must have been around then that Nell got pregnant.

Nell and I had stopped our tutoring sessions for the summer. In fact, Mr. Parshall had decided she was doing well enough at school to drop them entirely, but I told her I'd see her anyway, if she ever wanted. She was waitressing at a lunch place at the shopping center. In order to talk to her about the abortion, Anthony thought I might just show up for lunch there. He didn't know how else I could get to talk to her alone.

It was very busy, with so many customers that she didn't see me when I came in. She was efficiently going about her work with a tight face, her fluffy hair pulled back tight under a cap. I tried to figure out which was her area. Table by table she worked her way down the row to me.

"Mr. Stokes!" she said. She got nervous and blushed.

"I thought I should see how you were doing."

"Anthony told you," she said.

"Could we arrange another tutoring session, maybe, to—"

"Anthony wants you to convince me," she said.

"That's what he wants, but I just want to be sure you're talking to someone who can help."

"No one knows," she said, "except at the hospital when I had the test."

"Your mother?"

"My mother! Can I tell her anything?"

"Ruthie or Josie?"

"I can't tell anyone, Mr. Stokes. If no one knows, I can do something about it, and no one will ever know. I'm figuring out how to do something about it." After a moment's quiet, she said, "What do you want for lunch?"

I ordered a sandwich, and when she brought it she said, "Ladro's working in the More-For-Less at the other end of the parking lot. I have to walk the other way round not to see him each morning."

"Don't you want to get together and talk sometime, Nell?"

"There's that counselor I can talk to at the hospital."

"You've been?"

"She wants me to tell my parents."

"But about things between you and Anthony, that's what we could talk about."

"Anthony only sees it his way," she said. "We argue over and over. I tell him I won't do something about it right away, but I'm going to in a while. I'm going to decide. I'm not going to get married. I'm not going to have a baby. I have to go wait on other tables, Mr. Stokes."

When it got near the opening of school, and I had to be at meetings every day, Anthony was halfheartedly trying to decide what classes to take his first semester at the college downtown, but he could only think of Nell. I tried to see him, even if briefly, every evening at the library, where he'd gotten a custodial job. I don't know what made me tell him, once, what Ladro told me to tell him and then not to tell him. "He was kicking the wastebasket and saying how if there's ever anything in Anthony's life, he's going to take it away," I said.

"Ladro holds grudges," Anthony said quietly, sitting in the periodicals section during his break. "He won't beat me up. He'll try to take away something from me. I'll always be in fear of that, won't I."

"I shouldn't have told you."

"But I know how Ladro is. And you know what he might try to take? My baby."

"What!" I said, too loud for the library.

"I don't mean my baby with his own hands, but he might try to talk to Nell, convince her not to have it. She was working all summer at the shopping center where he worked too. She saw him sometimes on the sidewalk. It might be she'll go talk to him now, ask him what to do. She and I can't convince each other. We argue and argue. Maybe she'd rather talk to the person she used to love. She might think now he'd understand her better than I do. I can hear him, telling her it'd be all right to have an abortion."

"Ladro, the good Catholic?"

"Ladro holds grudges," Anthony said again.

"But Nell was afraid of running into him, when I saw her there at lunch."

"It still might happen," Anthony said.

"But now she's back at school, not working there. She wants nobody to know, Anthony, to make it easier for her."

"I want everybody to know," he said, too loud. A librarian peered at us over the frame of her glasses. Then he said quietly, changing the subject, "I'm writing something else, now that the Obloquy is finished. It's about my grandmother's death. It's about death. It's in memory of someone I never saw."

Those passages from the Obloquy came out in the Trochaic Review in September. I had a few advance copies on my desk at school. Isabel McGee, Liam's littlest sister, was a tenth grader now. Like Malinda, she hung around my desk the first day to explain who she was, and she flipped through the magazine while she waited for me to stop talking to some other student. She looked just like Liam, more than Malinda did. "It's not hard to spot a McGee," I said.

She turned slightly red. "This book you got there, it's got Anthony Ogna Santy in it. He went to this school, right? He was my brother's friend. That sort of looks like him," she said, opening to the picture of Og IX in the castle window.

"You're welcome to borrow a copy, Isabel." She said she would and proudly put the Trochaic Review on her stack of schoolbooks. I asked her as casually as I could where her brother was now.

"He got this job as an electrician," she said, "in Texas or somewhere."

"You don't have his address? Anthony might want to send him a copy," I said, hoping, Liam still somehow on my mind.

"Our mom doesn't know exactly where he is. Liam doesn't want to really be part of our family anymore. You think Liam's a bad kid, Mr. Stokes?"

"I never thought Liam was bad," I said, "but he had a rough time here."

"He told me I'd be lucky someday if I got to be in Mr. Stokes's class," Isabel said. "He comes by home when he was working for you, on your house and that, and he says you ought to see how it is at Mr. Stokes's house, it's not like here. It's like another world, he says."

Why did I feel, with each McGee, that they said nice things only to get something? Whenever I had a conference with Mrs. McGee she'd tell me in the stickiest friendly way how much I'd done to help her son and how grateful she was and was there anything she could do for me and on and on.

It was lonely at school beginning a year without Paula. I had no other colleague to talk to. The coordinator of the English curriculum, the French teacher, one of the guidance counselors—I'd have my businesslike lunches with them. Nell had begun her senior year, and I was the only person at school who knew she was pregnant.

After class a week later, Isabel McGee wanted to know what an obblecue was, and I found myself going into probably too much of an explanation. "What it's about," I said finally, "is his own father who died."

"His father and mother burnt up in a fire," Isabel said.

"And his father's the old king, I think, who kept his son in the castle tower, looking out a window, always alone. That boy was one of a long line of Ogs, and there was only one Umberto, but then he died, and the boy, who'd been beaten and starved, came down from the tower and found—"

"Like in a fairy tale," Isabel said. "But it's got all these words that don't make sense together." She read me some lines, exasperatedly: " 'This only   That when   Not enough Forgot   I not thinking   You not'—I don't get it, Mr. Stokes."

I picked up the copy and read on out loud, trying to put a natural stress on the phrases: " 'And everything dark as this   Something of walls resounding   Not you there in a cranny and chink and vines twining   And broken open fragile as it is   Can it be that in deep passages through stone   If again and again only echoes shadows planes far off.' " With each phrase she looked more bewildered.

"I don't make heads or tails of it, Mr. Stokes," she said.

"That's one of the harder parts."

"Is that what I'm supposed to be understanding in tenth-grade English?"

"I don't claim to understand it word for word," I said. "I only feel like I almost understand it, when I read it through at a sitting and let it settle."

"I give up," Isabel said, plopping down the Trochaic Review on my desk.

That evening at the library Anthony laughed to himself when I told him what Isabel had said. "You know what part I wish was printed instead of that one about shadows and echoes? The one where he comes out of the tower, the one about every bruise, every aching bone. I think that's a funny one."

"I found it scary," I said.

"Scary too," said Anthony, with another quiet laugh.

"Are you in a good mood tonight, Anthony?"

"Yes," he said and looked right at me, but something was wrong. "I'm not going to classes," he said.

"Anthony—"

"I went to the registrar and asked to have my admission deferred for what they call personal reasons."

"Anthony—"

"I can't go to classes now."

"But, Anthony—"

"I can only think about one thing, Burt, only one thing."

"But of all times when you could—"

"There'll be more time," he said, "if I get through this."

I had thought the worst time was over with the tears that night, but this was the beginning of the worst now, the fury I could see in his eyes. I began not to be able to think of anything else either. I began to teach like the others, distracted and mechanical. I didn't listen when my students read aloud in class, and I asked the wrong questions. I reduced my marginal comments to "Fine" and "Awkward" and "Needs Work" and didn't find time for private conferences. If Paula had been there—

I'd helped them move down in June but hadn't been to Providence since. And now I didn't want to leave town even for a day. I tried calling Paula at their apartment when Frank would be at the Trochee, and when I finally got her I tried to tell her everything that had happened. I even told her something of Liam, how companionable he'd really been, but since he'd left town, and even more of course since she and Frank had moved, I didn't know what to do with myself. "But don't tell Frank about Anthony and Nell," I told her. "I shouldn't even be telling you."

Paula listened and sympathized, and she kidded me around a bit to get me to act more like myself. A few days later I got this letter from her:

Dear Burt,

I don't write letters, but here's one. Your voice sounded shaky. Being away from teaching is doing me good. I think you should try it. Even planning it for next year would do you good. You're starting your eleventh year, and you've never had a sabbatical. Maybe you could even get the spring off. You should go away somewhere. (Italy, says Frank. I've talked to him about you, about this—not about Anthony's crisis, however—the subject of getting pregnant when you don't want to sits a little uncomfortably with Frank since we so far still haven't.)

Burt, it worries me how you live for those kids. I know they love you, but there are larger sources of love in this world. You have so few rewards all for yourself. You don't even expect rewards, and on that point I get a little annoyed. I suppose I could say you don't expect them, so you don't know what you're losing. But Burt, you're a grown man, nel mezzo del cammin (as Frank says), and I can't bear watching you stop.

Your instincts toward Anthony are fine and true. No doubt he needs you terribly, and Nell every bit as much. She's hoping you'll get through to Anthony, I'll bet, and help him in this bad time. But there's no reason for it to be a bad time in your life too. You haven't gotten anyone pregnant. You haven't lost your parents in a fire. Neither are you a promising young man of letters. Neither do you live in a cramped room in a depressing rooming house. You see, I'm a realist, aren't I!

You're a first-rate teacher and should probably be aiming for a job in a better school where you'll be appreciated more by your "superiors." (Your students appreciate you plenty, and you'll probably say that's all that matters.) And you should get the hell out of that beloved round house and start to work on a place that's yours! Mrs. C can only visit disappointment on you.

And please, Burt, don't lament Liam's departure. Of all the dependencies you've drifted into, that one has certainly the fewest rewards. So he's not quite the lame child I took him for. But Burt, you know that boy is out for trouble. He's a hard-bitten liar, if I may put it bluntly. I'd rather see you fostering a toughie like Ladro, who might pound the crap out of you, but I can tell you, he'll give it to you straight.

Do you know what little Liam said when I last encountered him (in the sub shop across from school sometime last spring)? "I was just over to school," he said, "seeing Burt, uh, Mr. Stokes, I mean, 'cause he's giving me special tutoring on Wednesdays, just 'cause he wants to, you know, 'cause he thinks I can pass the equivalency test, and then I'm going on to school in electronics."

"So he was giving you a session just now?" I asked, knowing full well you were going over the Colloquy with Anthony, because I'd just left Frank at the library and he was about to meet you two and pick up the manuscript.

"Yeah," said Liam. "You never thought I cared about studies, Mrs. Innocenzo, but I really did, and someday I'll show you how much

I been working and how far I got, even if I didn't graduate high school." I wished him luck. As much as he hated me, he just smiled, and lied and lied. I hate that in a kid more than anything. So what if he's good at stripping off wallpaper?

Will you please come down here and visit, Burt? Anthony's not going to attempt suicide, Nell's not going to have an abortion, not this weekend. So come down here. Get away from those kids. We love you too, but sometimes you take that for granted, won't put yourself out for us, won't try to make real adult friends. We're real adults, as real as you'll find, at least. But what kills me most is, of all my friends, you have the deepest powers of human understanding and practice them the least.

This is all out of love for you.

Paula

I had the excuse of meetings that weekend, and another excuse the next, and when I finally did go down it was for the Trochee party, and Anthony was with me.

He was in just the sort of state to make an impression on the bookstore crowd. If he had been his usual quiet self, he would have been ignored, taken for someone's shy kid. But Anthony, the Anthony I knew, was behaving slightly obnoxiously. We'd had a grim bus ride, when he hardly talked. He said he was only coming because I was making him. He didn't want to leave town, he was so sure Nell would do something irreparable. I promised we'd take the night bus back. He said he didn't want to see Paula and Frank the way he was feeling. I said they'd be preoccupied with the party and wouldn't notice. He didn't want to meet anybody who'd read his work. I said it was the least he could do for Frank, who'd done so much for him.

For the party, Frank had rented the loft upstairs from the Trochee. He and Kitchell had temporarily risen above their quarrel, and the Spondee people had all driven down in the Iambus. Kitchell, whom I'd never met before, had brought along the entertainment, a band he was sponsoring called Anna Pest and the Terrordactyls. When we came in, he and Frank were having a hearty disagreement over where to set them up.

Before Frank saw us, Paula came out of the bathroom with a handful of paper towels to mop up a beer she'd just spilled. She saw us and flung the paper towels in the air like huge confetti, shouting "Hurray!" Hugs, kisses—she almost had tears in her eyes to see us. We gathered the towels and helped her mop the spill. "I don't know why I'm so nervous as to knock over my first beer," she said. "She didn't look tired or puffy the way she used to after a rough week teaching. She looked slim, stylish even, in an elegant long blue dress instead of her flannel skirt and blouse.

"Here's our boy at last," said Frank, grabbing Anthony's shoulder and turning him around to introduce him to Kitchell, a spindle of a man in a three-piece tweed suit smoking a stubby pipe. Then he introduced me, and after formalities, Frank gave Anthony and me each a sudden bear hug. "Didn't think you'd make it to my party, boys," he said. "But Antonio—I said black tie, not black sweater."

Anthony wasn't in a jocular mood. He drank his first beer very fast, as I did mine. We were leaning against a wall, watching the party get going. "These people claim to read books!" he said to me, but much too loud. I pulled him over to Paula who, for a moment, had stopped handing out beers and wine.

"This is such an unsatisfactory way to see you," I said.

"At least you came," she said, poking my ribs.

"Burt made me come too," said Anthony.

"I don't suppose you cared to see us yourself, Anthony," said Paula, not quite aware of his mood.

"It isn't the same as it used to be," he said, a bit blurry. "You know, Paula, I'm not going to classes after all. I'm putting them off a while." Paula looked at me quickly to catch a sense of how much more desperate things might have become. "No—" Anthony began. "No, you know what? I'm not going to be a college student. I think I'm going to be a—" He waited a few seconds and then said: "—father." He turned around slowly and slipped into the crowd. I spent the next quarter hour talking more with Paula, she gripping my wrist and looking worried. Neither of us had an answer.

When the band started, no one could hear anything else. On another night I might have enjoyed watching them. The Terrordactyls had achieved the look that Liam seemed to strive for on Friday and Saturday nights. Anna Pest was a fat black woman dressed like a cleaning lady, old enough to be their mother. She jiggled about like a crazy woman, not what I'd call singing or dancing, but in a sort of whooping frenzy that for a while made me feel I was having a good time. The Terrordactyls just played their guitars and drums stiff-legged and stiff-armed, in their leather jackets and greasy jeans. During one song, Anna Pest grabbed a small whip and lashed at the three of them, yelping "Back! Back! Back!" A bookstore-type grabbed my elbow, and I could make out that he was trying to say something about metaphors. The whipping didn't faze the Terrordactyls.

I could see Anthony jumping in the crowd, dancing, but not with anyone. There were numerous lone dancers, in fact—people leaping wildly past each other, seldom face to face. I'm not a dancer of any sort, though Paula did try to coax me onto the floor during a quieter number called, if I heard it right, "I Ain't Had a Bite All Night."

When the band took a break, I found Anthony across the room with Kitchell. "Have you ever tried your hand at erotica?" Kitchell was asking him, drunk and dazed.

"I'm trying my hand at it this very moment," Anthony said.

"I'm sorry we can't do anything with the Obloquy right now—hello, Burt. I was saying we can't do anything with the Obloquy right now—it's a transitional period for us. But now Anthony says he's trying his hand at erotica."

Anthony looked at me, hardened, enjoying playing the trouble-maker.

"I'm sure the Monsignor will nonetheless find something spiritual in it," I said.

"Well, religious erotica's the best kind, with nuns in it," said Kitchell, not knowing what we were talking about. Then Anna Pest stepped over to his side. "Oh, here's Sarah. Sarah Bowen: Anthony Ognissanti, our young fabulist, and his friend Burt something. What did you two make of Sarah's impersonation?"

I certainly didn't know what to say. Sarah Bowen had a long critical piece in the first Trochaic Review with Anthony, and now it seemed she was Anna Pest on the side.

"It was such a lark!" she said with a wide smile. "Kitchell heard the boys in one of the clubs he frequents and hired them just for me, tonight, so I could realize my life's ambition to make a public fool of myself. This uniform belonged to my mother once."

"It's only the beginning," said Kitchell.

"You're great," said Anthony. "You wrote the songs?"

" 'Wrote' is kind. Mere improvisation," she said, smoothing her apron. "The boys played their usual instrumentals, and I just got up and did what I did."

"I thought it was the real thing," I finally said.

"You asshole, Burt," said Anthony, "what do you want for it to be real?"

"You asshole, Anthony," I said back, feeling improvisatory myself.

"So you're Ognissanti," said Sarah Bowen, taking his hand and turning serious. "I'd been expecting you to sign up for my advanced seminar. Kitchell told me you'd definitely be taking it."

"This boy is putting off college for a while," I said.

Kitchell stretched his arms out, one on my shoulder, one on Sarah Bowen's. Anthony stood facing the three of us and said, "I need a beer," and off he went.

"Sarah dear—excuse me, Burt—Sarah dear," said Kitchell as he dropped the arm from my shoulder and sauntered off with her out of my hearing.

The Terrordactyls started up again, without Anna Pest, and it was much too loud. I couldn't hear Anthony when I found him, and he didn't listen to me. Frank, the only black tie in sight, was talking at everyone, one after another, proud of the gathering he'd organized. Paula looked sadder to me as it got later. "We could go for a walk," I mouthed at her as clearly as I could.

On the sidewalk, in the quiet and cold, we walked randomly around blocks, not the best of neighborhoods, and soon she was telling me how worried she was that she hadn't gotten pregnant, that she didn't know what to do, that they were keeping at it because it was just that Frank's sperm count was low. "This sperm count business is something I've never given much thought to," I said.

It's now more than a year that they've been trying, and there's still nothing. In her last letter, Paula writes that they're thinking of adopting now. She's getting too old to wait any longer, to hope for it. Paula, who said she didn't write letters, writes me because I still don't go see her and Frank, and we find it awkward on the phone, both of us. Nell's even a little jealous of my letters from Paula.

On our walk we stopped in a bar to warm us up. I knew I was drinking more than I was accustomed to, and so was she. Looking at her across the table, I had the odd thought of what if we made a sort of arrangement, that I would sleep with her and get her pregnant for Frank, who'd never have to know. Luckily, I wasn't drunk enough to tell the idea to Paula, but I kept thinking it, drunkenly, the rest of the evening. On the night bus home, alone, I worked out a lengthy happy fantasy about it. It seemed a practical thing to do. The child would be Umberto Innocenzo, I decided, and I would keep my secret for life, my identity hidden in his name. As I fell half asleep I wasn't sure if I wouldn't really tell Paula about it, what a good idea it seemed.

I had to walk the four miles home from the downtown bus station because the local buses didn't run that late and I didn't have money for a cab. I'd left Anthony in Providence. When it had come time to catch the last bus, I'd tried to extricate him from the party, but he was reeling about with a bunch of people who knew him only as the young author of those fragmentary phrases in the Obloquy. I stood watching him a while, and it looked like that coronation scene. What a strange costume party for Og IX! Who were those people waving pennants and dancing? In a church? I blinked awake.

"Get yourself home then, you stupid fuck," I said, a way I'd never spoken to him before.

"I'm going back with them all in the Iambus," he said. "Sarah'll take me. I'm having a great time. You mad, Burt?"

I didn't bother to go see Anthony at the library Monday or Tuesday evening. On Wednesday, at lunch with one of the guidance counselors, I heard that the parents of yet another senior girl had taken their daughter out of school, obviously because she was pregnant.

"When something like that happens," I said, assuming it was

Nell, "shouldn't the school take some responsibility to look into it? What if the parents were, let's say, forcing her somehow—"

He wondered if I had any idea how many cases he saw like that. I put on the helpless smile we all put on at school when we thought about the way things were.

Anthony was at the round house sitting on the front step when I got home at four. He was shivering in the late October wind, despite both sweaters, the bulky black one over the blue one with the darned elbow. He didn't say anything. I put the key in the lock and let him in. I turned up the heat and put a pot of water on. "Coffee?" I said.

"I'm never drinking beer again," he said from the living room. When I brought him a hot mug, he said, "I was supposed to meet Nell yesterday at the library, Burt, but she didn't come. I decided I had to call her at home. Mr. Parshall answered the phone. 'We think it's you,' he kept saying. 'It's you or Ladro Brown, see, but we think it's you. You'd better not come around here, see,' he said, and he said they locked Nell in her room, and then he hung up. They locked Nell in her room! I kept thinking I'd go rescue her as soon as I left work, but I just went home. I didn't know what to do. Miss Burnham saw me come in. She had me in for some beer, and I got drunk again, Burt, and tried to explain to her—When I went to my room, I just passed out."

He was on the couch, head up on the arm, sipping from his mug. I was in my big chair with mine. This was the last long talk I had alone with Anthony.

"I woke up early today," he said. "I sat and stared all morning. I played downstairs with the dog. Then I came over here and waited. What am I waiting for, Burt? What am I going to do?"

"Are they locking her up to keep her from getting an abortion, Anthony, or locking her up to make sure she gets one and doesn't run away?"

"Nell had to give them all her money from waitressing. She wanted me to use some of the money from my grandmother. The money just came through. Either I gave Nell the money in one week or that was it, she'd go to her parents, because it's already two and a half months she's pregnant. But it's not been a week, Burt. I still had till Friday."

He put his mug down and stared at the ceiling. I saw him twisting his lips, squinting his eyes. With his fists he began to pound his forehead, asking what was he going to do, what was he going to do.

"Why don't you talk to Brother Nor now," I said, afraid to say it, "because I don't—"

"No, no, no, no—" Anthony kept pounding his forehead.

"Could you go to confession?" I asked.

"No, no—" And on and on.

"Wouldn't it help? Go over here to Saint Ursula's instead. Don't go to Saint Vincent's if you don't want to."

Anthony kept saying no. Then he said, "Confess I slept with Nell? I'm talking about what's going to happen. You don't confess that. What's there to do but go get Nell, steal her out her window—"

"You can't make her have a baby, Anthony."

"If I bring her here, Burt, will you keep her?"

"Keep?"

"Let her stay?"

"If she wants to—"

"Everything has to do with if she wants to!"

"What you want more than what she wants?"

"No!" Anthony yelled at me, sitting right up. "Not what I want. What's taught us to do by God's love."

Anthony had never put anything that way to me. I didn't even think of him as having such a feeling. For me, it was because his mother and father died in the fire that he couldn't bear to let something die, born or not.

"Go to the Monsignor, please, Anthony," I said. "If you can't go to Brother Nor, go to the Monsignor. He knows the limits of what you can do now. I'm no help to you in this."

"But you'll let Nell stay here," he said, then added, "if she wants to."

I found myself scared by what I was letting myself do. Why did it seem more dangerous than all the things I'd ever done with Liam? After Anthony left, I had to take my mind off it by vacuuming every floor in the round house. And quite late that evening, in the rain, Anthony was there at the door with Nell in a plaid bathrobe, both soaking. His sneakers were on her feet and he was barefoot. I boiled a pot of water and made them each a footbath to warm them and wrapped them in quilts, side by side on the couch. I only asked, "How did you do it?"

"I did what Liam used to do. I never thought I could do it," Anthony said. He was excited, despite chattering teeth. "I pulled myself up the back porch of her house and climbed around on a side roof and got to her window."

"Didn't that scare you, Nell?"

"She wasn't scared. She got up and opened the window. She didn't let me in. She climbed out after me."

"You both might've been killed slipping from the roof."

"And in this rain!" said Anthony, exhilarated. "Then, Burt, I got her down the back porch. She hung by her hands from the railing and I had her ankles, then she just dropped and slid down, with my arms coming up around her."

"For a girl who's pregnant—"

"And then we ran, but around the corner we stopped and I gave her my sneakers."

I asked Nell why her parents had locked her in.

"She hasn't told me," Anthony said.

"Nell?"

"It was stupid," she finally said.

"She was waiting till Friday, but then—"

"I'll tell it, Anthony," she said. She looked up from that brown quilt, tilting her head at me. "It was stupid. My mother buys my Kotex, see, and so she goes to see when I need a new box, and the same new one she bought two months ago is sitting there and I haven't opened it. First she thinks I'm using Tampax now and not telling her. That's bad enough. So she goes through my drawers. She goes through everything. Then she begins to really wonder, and she remembers how I was being sick at the beginning of school this year and she figures it out, and so I tell her it's true."

"And what do they want you to do?"

"I'm out of school right off," said Nell. "They're going to send me to Saint Ursula's for the rest of the year when this is over. But first I'm having the abortion. It's Monday next week."

"Saint Ursula's would like that," said Anthony with a laugh.

"But why are they locking you in?" I still wanted to know.

"You ask them," said Nell. "You think they trust me? My father?"

I said they should both take hot baths. Nell went up first. I pulled out of the bottom drawer in the dining room some jeans and a sweatshirt Liam had left behind, which would fit her well enough, and a splotchy pair of his sneakers he wore for painting. I piled them outside the bathroom door, and in a while Anthony went up too, and I waited downstairs. He didn't seem to have a plan for what to do next. I wondered if they were making love in the tub, or maybe just playing, to make each other happy again. I didn't want to hear, so I turned the TV on, something I never do.

After the bath, they came downstairs, his arm around her. And now, each night on our couch in the living room, Nell goes over it again and again when we talk. She thinks that was when she could have rescued Anthony. I'd opened some cans and heated up a late night supper of stew for them. We sat at the kitchen table on the stools the way it had been a year before when they were falling in love, and it came back to the naming of babies, how he didn't like Umberto, how if it was a girl she would be Clara. Anthony must have thought it was decided she wouldn't have the abortion.

Now Nell thinks she should have said nothing. "I should have faked it, Burt," she said a few nights ago. "All that climbing over roofs, later I could've pretended to have a miscarriage. He'd've believed that."

"You said what you had to say, Nell," I told her. "He was dreaming of his baby, named by him, of his fatherhood. We'll always love Anthony, Nell, but we'll have to think of him as an eighteen-year-old forever, and we'll get older and older. He didn't live beyond the selfishness of his youth."

"He was the same age I am now," said Nell.

"Nell," I said, "do you know that you're an adult? It's not just what you've been through. It's been in you all along. You never were selfish. You loved someone."

"Why did I decide to stay pregnant after he died, Burt? It was funny to have a baby inside. When Anthony died, she was suddenly there. And you do love her, before you know her. And after she's born you go to take a bath maybe while she's sleeping, and you lie in the tub by yourself and you almost forget she's out there sleeping. You're just yourself for a while. I didn't know what it'd be like to have a baby there. From before when she was born, I think I loved her inside me already. And at first when she was nursing—I didn't know before what it'd be like. Back with Anthony, I didn't know either, but still the part of you that wanted an abortion, it's bound to stay too, isn't it, Burt, and make you feel you don't want to have this baby that's always there with you, so that taking a bath you don't forget long—"

"Yes, Nell, yes, Nell," I said, touching her fluffy hair on my shoulder.

"So what I said to him that night, how I didn't want Clara and I didn't want Umberto, even if I liked Umberto for a name, and how I didn't want his baby now, or to get married, and how I said my parents had the wrong way of doing it but they were right, and if he still wanted a baby with me in a couple of years, then we'd have one—"

"And he said you'd been talking to Ladro, and you said so what if you had, though you hadn't been."

"But I did sort of talk once to Ladro," she said. "I went by the More-For-Less after school. There were lots of people, and he pretended he didn't see me. I went over to him where he was making duplicate keys on that little machine. He said hi, and I just asked what would he do if he got a girl pregnant."

"You went and asked him that?"

"It's somehow like we were just talking the day before, like nothing happened. He looks at me, just filing off the key, and he asks if Ruthie told me so. I say told me what. He says that someone might be pregnant and Ruthie knows about it and it could've been him that did it. 'You!' I say, because he's the one that never wanted to go that far. 'It could've been,' he says. I figure it's Josie. 'None of your business,' says Ladro. I'm asking just about what would he do, like if it was just anybody. 'I'd do what she wanted,' Ladro says. Get married? 'Yeah.' Get money for an abortion? He says, 'Whatever she wants.' Is that what he's going to do? 'Yeah,' he says."

"Which?"

"I don't know what he did," Nell said. "I don't know who it was, or if he was just talking. The lady came for her key. I just went on and left. Why wouldn't Anthony do what I wanted is what I kept thinking. And then my mother finds the full box of Kotex the next day."

This was Nell's last fight with Anthony:

"Just because you rescue me from them doesn't mean I change my mind."

"You've probably been talking to Ladro."

"So what if I did?"

"If you're listening to him about having a baby, you know what he's going to tell you. He doesn't want you to have anything with me."

"You don't know anything, Anthony."

"I know more than you."

"You don't know what I want. You rescue me from my house, you think. I'm going to the hospital next week myself. I don't care if my parents are there or if you're there too."

"You're going to stay here, Nell," said Anthony. "We can go down to Monsignor. I'm going first and tell him everything. Then you'll come. We have to go there, Nell. We'll do what he says, Nell."

"I don't care what you'll do."

"Her parents must be looking for her, Anthony," I said.

"She can hide here," he said. I don't think it seemed possible to him anymore but some story he'd made up that he wanted to be true. "The third floor, no one will find her, or the basement—"

Nell stood up from the table. "I know how to get back in our basement window. I can sneak up to the porch and over the roof." She walked into the hall. We came with her. Rain plopped on the dark skylight way above us.

"Where are you going?" Anthony said, almost crying. She was going to the door and opening it. He grabbed her shoulder from behind and shook her, saying no, no, no— He tried to pull her to him. She tried to bite his hand to make him let go, and he hit at her face, reaching his other hand around from behind her. Then he stood still. She walked on out the door and slammed it. I found myself shaking. He turned around to me, and much too late, several seconds after he hit her, I hit him on his face with my palm. I stared at him.

"Hit me all over, Burt," he said, "like my father."

"I'm sorry, Anthony."

"I hit Nell," he said slowly, staring. "Where are my sneakers?"

I found them in the kitchen, warming on the stove. "Don't go to her house, Anthony."

"No," he said, "I'll go to my room. I'll think. I'll go to Monsignor tomorrow. I'll go to Monsignor."

"Call me, tell me," I said. "But if you want to come here and stay, there's a room for you—"

He put his sneakers on at the door. "No, I want to go to my room."

"Why did I hit you?" I said. I was still shaking. I could feel it through all of me.

"I'm going, Burt," he said. "I'll come back to you—" His muffled words at the door as he opened it and slipped out—

On Thursday I knew how much I hated it at school now. Isabel McGee must have wondered what it was her brother had told her to look forward to in Mr. Stokes. No call from Anthony that night—I hoped the Monsignor, or Brother Nor, would be making all better. And then all day Friday, which was Halloween, no call. I had some candy bars in case neighborhood kids came by. A few did. And then later there was a furious pounding on my door. I opened, scared, and a fat boy was gasping, "Let me in, let me in, please, please, quick!" As I closed the door behind him, an egg hit the door and then a couple more. "They're chasing," he said, catching breaths. He didn't have a costume, not even a mask, just a paper bag for candy. It was the same boy who'd ridden by on his bike when I was first asking about the house and he'd said it was round, yeah, it was round.

"Why are they chasing you?" I asked.

"They always beat on me at school," he said. "They're hiding in the bushes."

"Should I call your father to come?"

"He doesn't live here."

"Your mother?"

"My mom's out."

"Is there anybody?"

"Let me stay till they give up," he said. "I won't bother you, sir."

I gave him the candy bars that were left. He sat on the bottom step of the staircase, sorting through his bag. "Sorry about the eggs on your door," he said. I went back to wash dishes, and then I sat at the table with a book and waited to hear from Anthony. In a while the boy decided it was safe to leave.

"So you live here," he said at the door. "The old lady sell it to you?"

"She still owns it."

"Everytime I ride by her house," he said, "she leans out and yells at me. I always say Fucka You Mama to her. Well, thanks, sir."

I wiped the door clean with my dish towel. It was calming down to a cold clear night. I thought of calling Brother Nor. I thought of walking out, over the hill, to see if Anthony's light was on. But I went in and waited by the phone, reading. I looked at the clock at eleven, and not all that much later, it seemed, at twelve. It was just after twelve that Anthony was hit by the last bus of the night heading downtown past the town hall, the high school, the library.

The phone rang in the night, and I jumped up from bed, afraid right away. "Anthony," I said aloud, grabbing at the receiver.

'Mr. Stokes," said Brother Nor's voice, "Anthony's had an accident. He's here at the hospital, but they don't know if they'll save him."

"Brother Nor—"

"Please come," said Brother Nor.

I ran uphill to a cross street that went through, then along and down to the hospital. Brother Nor was right there in the dim lobby, in his soutane with a gray parka over it, walking up and down. He saw me and came and grasped both my hands, tears to the brims of his eyes.

"Anthony—" I said, but Brother Nor couldn't talk. I went to the night nurse behind the desk.

"Are you Mr. Stokes, his teacher?" she asked. "They'll do all they can, but he even may be gone now. Do you know what happened?"

"No," I said.

"He ran out in front of the bus, there by the town hall. He leaped right in front of it. He was flung forward, and the bus couldn't stop that quick, so it hit him again. He was about gone when they got him here. It was an awful thing to have to see." She had eyes that saw how stunned I was, and she tried to tell me clearly, firmly, leaving feeling to me.

I didn't see Anthony. Brother Nor had seen him, and blessed him, and a priest from Saint Ursula's around the corner gave the last rites. Then Brother Nor had called me. He had no one else to call because the Monsignor was out of town for a few days. We sat on a red vinyl couch with metal-tube arms, like the doctor's waiting-room couches of my childhood. All the time we sat, Brother Nor's eyes were brimming but not crying, and I sat without a word to say in my mind, without moving. I thought a word was coming to me, but it would fall back before I knew what it would have been.

Brother Nor told me things: "He went to Monsignor yesterday. Monsignor called me and said I must take special care of Anthony with him out of town. He said Anthony would tell me what was wrong, but Anthony didn't come to me. Monsignor said Anthony's troubles are with him still. He said we have a lot of work to do, and we need hope. He said to me, 'Our hope comes partly from Anthony. When we see all that God has given him, how can we not hope?' He said Anthony would come to me, but he didn't. Why was he up on the hill in the night? Was he going home or going the other way, to you? Or was he going to come down his old street, see if my light was on, since it always is? I sit up reading every night late, Mr. Stokes."

The nurse, who'd gone down the hall, came back, first to the desk to write something, then over to us. She stood before us, breasts like two big stones. "They've washed him off, closed his eyes. You may both go in and see the dead boy."

Brother Nor stood, but I sat. I couldn't get up. She went with him down the hall. Only when I was there alone could I begin to make a sound, catching in my throat. I went out the door and walked along the streets of our dark town, which seemed to have been abandoned—shambly old buildings, wires everywhere overhead, all the cement, the chain-link fences, three-deckers street after street.

Then it was Monday. I hadn't talked with anyone, except Brother Nor again, who called to tell me when the funeral was. He had arranged everything, even called the Innocenzos. All I could say was thank you.

Paula and Frank came first to the round house to pick me up, and we walked over the hill to Saint Vincent's Church and in the tall doors. Paula and Frank crossed themselves, then knelt in a pew, and I slipped in next to them and sat. It was a rather plain church, white plaster, dark wood around the narrow windows, dark altar, dark pulpit, floor of stone. High iron chandeliers hung from chains, like crowns, two by two. I hadn't been in a church since I'd left home years back. This wouldn't be like my Catholic grandfather's funeral, Latin Requiem, bells, incense swinging around the coffin.

Paula touched my elbow and nodded at the young woman passing down the aisle on a young man's arm. Elsa, I thought. I only just saw her face, but then all her dark hair, and I could remember the back of her head working at her desk in my classroom, the first one there as I came in each morning. I couldn't see Martin Keeney's face, only his trim hair, his dark suit, and I still couldn't recall him. They didn't cross themselves or kneel but took the front pew, and then I noticed the row of small heads just behind them, with Brother Nor at the far end, boys from the Saint Vincent Home. Behind them were teachers and some high school students and people I didn't recognize who must have known Anthony through the church. I recognized two librarians and off to one side, alone, Miss Burnham. Kitchell was there with Sarah Bowen and some other Spondee people, but we didn't talk to them. The McGees were there with Malinda and Isabel. When would Liam find out what had happened to his old friend? Of course the Parshalls were not there. Brother Nor told me he had called them, but they wouldn't talk to him. I should have gone to their door, insisted Nell be allowed to come to the church with me. I hadn't done a thing but sit in my loneliness. What was Nell going through alone?

Six of the older boys from the Home brought the coffin down the aisle. One of them could have been that chubby boy Anthony had pushed down the stairs. They all sniffed as the organ played something that seemed tuneless. Then there was the Monsignor, whom I felt I knew. He was small, with glasses, bald with a bit of gray fringe. His voice turned out to be deep and warm, as I had imagined, but he was not the tall stern bishop of Frank's coronation scene, the only way I'd been picturing him till then.

Toward the end of the mass, before the prayer to the Lamb of God, if I remember the forms that meant nothing to me from the farthest past, I saw to one side of the altar a boy sit down with a cello, and he began a tune I knew, Panis Angelicus, and the organ played along. Then on the other side, by the organ, another boy stood up and began to sing it. Paula had been holding Frank's arm, and she reached for mine, holding it too. The tune came back to me with each phrase. That was when I would have wanted to cry. I heard a gruff sobbing in the row behind us, and the voice of the boy, and the singing cello. Pauper, pauper, servus et humilis—they were words I remembered. I turned to see Paula's tears, and I glanced just behind her, and there was Ladro Brown, with his head in his hands, shaking with his sobs.

The burial was at the cemetery where the Ognissantis were buried. Paula and Frank and I couldn't bring ourselves to go on to it. On our slow walk back to the round house, Paula said, "I want you to burn that awful letter I wrote you, where I said Anthony wasn't going to attempt suicide or Nell have an abortion. How could I have written that?"

"You loved Anthony, Paula. You can't feel bad for anything you wrote. We've all written things like that in letters." I hadn't said as many words at once in two days.

"Paula feels so guilty for that letter," Frank said.

At the top of the hill, we stopped walking and looked at each other, because this was where the bus had gone. We hadn't thought of it walking over because we'd all been so much in our thoughts. Now Frank reached out and held the signpost for the bus stop, squeezed it hard to hold himself up.

On the phone Brother Nor had told me what he found out the bus driver had told the police. The boy hadn't been looking, had just been running, and it was in my direction, up over the hill from his side. No one thought he had meant to kill himself. But in those days before the funeral I had been thinking how scared Anthony had been. He could have been coming back to see me. Or he might have had some more beer with Miss Burnham and got drunk again and wandered along the streets thinking he wanted to die. He might have started running, maybe as if he was running to a burning house again, not caring if anything hit him, running just to see if he would live through it. That way Anthony would put himself in what he thought of as God's hands. Was he offering a life for a life?

I wondered if I should try to find Elsa after the funeral and talk to her. I even called the only Keeney in the phone book, but it wasn't the same family. At the high school I looked up old yearbooks for a clue to Martin. I had had so many students since that I didn't recognize the pale shadowless face in the picture. So I stopped thinking of him and Elsa. It was months later, after Antonia was born, that her warning letter came. Nell and I read it together on the couch, with the baby sleeping between us in her white blanket. Nell proudly pointed out Elsa's spelling mistakes.

Mr. Stokes,

I found out what you did. An aunt of Martin still lives there and she found out since her sister-in-law works at the hospital. I can't believe it. You know who I am. You remember me, that's for sure. What do you think your doing taking Anthony's baby? I saw you back at the funeral, and Miss McCune too. I know Anthony said you and her were his best teachers and you really taught him a lot so I don't hold that against you. But I heard some things from that man Kitchell when I was there. He came and told me about Anthony's books and how you tried to get Anthony to go to some publisher where Miss McCune's husband works, whatever his name is. Anyway that man Kitchell says Anthony was a young genius and his books are going to be famous. So what happened is I sent him all the letters Anthony wrote and he thinks there the most beautiful thing Anthony ever wrote. Now he's made a book with parts I wrote about what

Anthony was like. And you never thought I could write in school. So that's coming out and then you'll see what Anthony really wanted. You'll see what really happened to him. You don't know anything. What did you do? Think he wanted you to marry that girl for him? I can't believe you did that with a senior girl. We just found all this out because of Martin's aunt. And you named her Antonia. There's one thing for sure is that Anthony always wanted a baby Clara. You know about what happened to our parents. That was our mother's name Clara. How can you call her Antonia? Now let me tell you its not going to just stay like that with you bringing up his kid. You think I'm just not going to actully do something about it, but Martin's going east for his company and then you'll see. I'm not giving up. And you think that young girls going to stay with you and bring up that kid? Your crazy she is. Whose going to bring up Clara? That's why I and Martin want her. We are her aunt and uncle. We can give her so much because Martin's got a great job and we live in a great place for a kid. I want that baby coming to me and somehow its going to happen. You think I don't dare. Maybe not me but you wait till Martin comes, then your in for a surprise for sure. You think you can take Anthony's baby, well maybe someone can take her back so don't be to sure. And Kitchell says he's going to get back that new book of Anthony's from that other guy because he's Anthony's official publisher. And you know I get the money from those books. And from the letters too. So don't Nell or you try to get any even if you say its for Clara or we'll take you to court. Martin's aunt gave us your address.

Elsa Keeney

"She must be in another strange period, like after the death of their parents," I said, hoping the letter was too stupid to worry Nell.

"What's this book of letters?" Nell asked, staring down at the baby.

"I can't imagine it'll come off," I said, knowing already through Frank that Kitchell was rushing it out that month, but I wanted to see it first to be sure it wouldn't upset her. In a few weeks, after Antonia was gone and Nell would hardly talk, I knew I had to keep that book from her for as long as I could.

"His sister thinks she knows everything about Anthony," Nell said, "but he said he could never live with her. She'd drive him crazy."

"We don't have to worry about Elsa," I said. "There's nothing Martin can do. Everything is legal now."

"And this is our baby Antonia no matter what Elsa thinks," Nell said.

Whatever I'd lost not teaching was nothing to me beside that baby I'd never hoped to have. If we still had Antonia now, what love would be growing between us? Would the nights I spend with Nell be different, with the baby asleep on the other side of our wall, instead of in between our separate rooms? We might even be thinking we should have another baby, not yet, but it would be a thought. The last I saw of Antonia was her little dark eyes, darker each day, looking at me from her crib, and then they closed and she slept, and Nell and I snuck out of the room and shut the door without making a sound.

Tuesday after the funeral I had to go back to teaching, but everyone at school knew I was out of myself, only doing what I had to. Paula had said she would stay with me for a few days to keep me from that bad way, but I didn't think Frank would like it, and I didn't want Paula there—I wanted my loneliness. I knew that I had had nothing of my own for many years, perhaps always. And Liam was gone, too. It made me feel almost truer to be myself alone. I didn't want to sit in my big comfortable chair or sleep in my warm bed. I sat in the kitchen on a stool and slept between my two quilts on the hard floor. I kept the heat low. I didn't read a book. I ate bread and soup only. On that cold Friday night, Nell came to me.

She was bundled in sweaters and skirts and socks, on top of each other. She couldn't stop talking as soon as I opened the door. "My parents took all the shoes out of my room," she said, "and my parka and my winter jacket. I put on everything left I could. It made it softer if I fell. I did what I did with Anthony, but I had to break the window because they nailed it. I waited till a fire engine was going right by our street so they wouldn't hear the glass break. And no one was there to catch me like Anthony when I hung off the porch, but I aimed for a bunch of garbage bags."

I looked at her closely in all the layers. "Nell, are you still pregnant?"

"I wouldn't have the abortion. I told them I wouldn't. They were so stupid to tell me Anthony was killed. I wouldn't have found out because they were keeping me in my room till the hospital. Then I would've had the abortion. But they wanted to find out if it was Anthony like they thought. I didn't believe them till they showed me the newspaper. Then I went crazy in front of them. I didn't stop to think what to say. I just said I was going to have the baby. 'See, it was him,' says my father. I wouldn't say anything. They thought I'd calm down and get over it about the abortion, then they realized I wouldn't, so they locked me in again. But on Monday I wouldn't go to the hospital. They even got me there, but I wouldn't have the abortion. They can't force you to have an abortion even if you're seventeen."

"Nell—" I said, holding her shoulders because as she talked she got so tense. "How did you ever bear it in that room alone, locked in, knowing Anthony was dead—"

"It was the day of his funeral they took me to the hospital. The counselor there understood. My parents just said well, we're going home then and we'll be back."

"And even then they kept you locked in?"

"They took out all my shoes and nailed the window."

"But why, Nell? What were they trying to do to you?"

"I was even afraid they'd get some doctor to come to the house and make me have one."

"Why couldn't they let you have the baby?"

"They say I have to get married. 'And that kid Anthony's dead,' my father says. 'It wasn't him anyway,' I say, because I don't want them talking that way about Anthony. I don't want to ever see them again. Anthony said you'd hide me—"

I decided I would go to the hospital in the morning, to the counselor there, for advice, perhaps even go to the police. It was a case of abuse, it had to be. I would certainly risk keeping Nell for a night.

Because she hadn't talked to anyone for so long, she wasn't ready for bed then, but I made up the couch with quilts, brought her the plaid bathrobe she'd left on that rainy night, and went out to the all-night corner store to get some muffins because she was hungry. She curled around me on the couch as we ate, and she told me how she had cried alone in her room for days. Then she asked me to tell her what I knew about Anthony's death and about the funeral. That evening, I came back into myself.

In the morning, when Nell was still asleep, I got a call from Mrs. McGee. "Mr. Stokes, this is Isabel McGee's mother. You'll think this is an odd thing to call about. I don't know if you know the Parshall family? They had a daughter in the school a year ahead of Malinda? I think they just took her out?"

"Nell Parshall," I said.

"I just received a call from Mrs. Parshall, Mr. Stokes. I have her on my list at the church. She does refreshments. In any case, she found my son's clothes with his name tapes in them in her daughter's room. I couldn't imagine what to say. I think Isabel told you, Mr. Stokes, Liam's working in Texas now, and of course he hasn't been back here. Her implying he could've gotten their daughter pregnant, well, you were such an intimate coun-selor to Liam, you know how unlikely that is!"

"Mrs. Parshall said their daughter was pregnant?" I asked, carefully.

"She was implying so, and she thought I might know where her daughter could be. With my son perhaps? I said my son's in Texas. She wanted his number, but I didn't give it to her."

It occurred to me, even in the midst of this, to take advantage of the chance to find out where Liam was, but when I said I could call him and ask what was behind Nell having his clothes, Mrs. McGee said he didn't have a phone at the moment because he was on the road a lot. "What I thought, Mr. Stokes, was that these clothes of Liam's, well, Mrs. Parshall said the sneakers had spatters of paint on them, and somehow they might have gotten from your house, when he was working for you, to Nell Parshall? The reason I'm calling is really to warn you you'll be hearing from Mrs. Parshall this morning, and I want to explain it to you, so you won't think I was implying you had anything to do with this. It's so unpleasant to deal with when we're all so sad over the Ogna Santy boy."

I didn't want to hear more from Mrs. McGee, so I thanked her and hung up and rushed downstairs to wake up Nell.

"And I could've worn those sneakers last night instead of all those socks!" she said. "I forgot about them under my bed. I hid them after I snuck back in that night."

We heard a car stop on the street. Nell looked up and jumped from the quilts in her T-shirt and underpants, wrapped the blue quilt around her and ran to the stairs. I looked out the window behind the couch and saw over the bushes the blue light on a police car and Mr. Parshall's head and shoulders coming around the passenger's side. A policeman and a policewoman were coming up my walk, Mr. Parshall a few steps behind. I bundled all of Nell's clothes into the brown quilt and ran to the dining room, pulled out the bottom drawer and stuffed the clothes into the pie-shaped wasted space, where I keep the pictures of Liam. The doorbell rang, and I folded the quilt into the empty drawer and slid it back in.

I opened my door. "Mr. Parshall," I said, "has something happened to Nell?"

He didn't answer. "Burt Stokes?" said the policewoman, and I nodded. "There's a complicated situation we need your help with, because you taught all these kids. You taught the boy who was killed a week ago, you taught this man's daughter, and her mother says you also taught a boy named Liam McGee."

We stood in the center hall with light falling down to us. "You've done a beautiful job on this place," said the policeman. I wanted to move them on to the living room, away from the stairs, which the policeman was admiring, following the curve of the bannister with his eyes, where Nell had run.

"We have two separate situations, but they seem connected," the policewoman said. "Nell Parshall and Liam McGee are both runaways. Liam McGee has been missing for some time, or rather it seems his parents haven't known where he is, to put it their way. Nell Parshall has been missing since last night, and she left behind some clothes that belonged to Liam McGee."

"Mrs. McGee just called me," I said. "I know about the clothes. They sound like clothes Liam wore when he was working here for me." Mr. Parshall was looking at me, tired and scared.

"Mrs. Parshall doesn't know how she got the clothes," the policewoman said. "You may have heard from her guidance counselor that Nell's pregnant, and her parents believe the boy who was killed to have been her boyfriend, though she wouldn't tell them if he got her pregnant. But after he was killed, her parents tell us, she refused to have the abortion she'd previously agreed to."

"Have you seen her, Mr. Stokes?" Mr. Parshall said.

"She wasn't at the funeral," I said. It came to me, in all this, that I hated him for not letting Nell go to the funeral. I began not to worry for myself.

The policewoman went on: "At the same time we're looking into Liam McGee. The city police arrested a man downtown last summer who ran a sort of call service for businessmen, and he had a portfolio of pictures of his girls and boys. I don't know if you ever counseled Liam on this side of his life, Mr. Stokes. We spoke to his parents several months ago, and it was no news to them, but they said how he was nineteen now and off on his own somewhere else, they admitted they didn't know exactly where. But these clothes turning up made us wonder if he hadn't come back here or if there wasn't some connection with Nell Parshall. Could he have got her somehow involved, for instance, with this call service last summer, and perhaps that's how she got pregnant—"

"It couldn't be that," said Mr. Parshall very quietly, "could it, Mr. Stokes? You know Nell—"

"When did you last see these clothes?" the policewoman asked me. The policeman looked over from examining the door moldings and realized he should pull the clothes out of the satchel he was carrying. There were the white name tapes with Liam McGee on them in red.

"He stopped working here sometime at the beginning of last summer," I said.

"I can't get over this staircase," said the policeman. "Could I run up and take a look from above? This is a gem of an old house. Driving by, I always wanted to see it inside."

"It's not finished up there," I said, but I didn't dare ask him not to. I was sure they had it set up, their method of investigating in apparent innocence. I hoped Nell was hidden under the bed.

Mr. Parshall asked if he could sit down in the kitchen a minute. I offered to make coffee. "We'll be going," said the policewoman, "but let me ask one more thing her parents weren't sure about. Who were Nell's closest friends at school, where she might have gone?"

I said I was under the impression that she'd drifted away from her friends that fall, but I gave her Ruthie's name and was about to give her Josie's when the policeman called from above: "She's here, Anne!" The policewoman ran up the stairs. Nell had run all the way to the third floor and was wrapped in the quilt under the stepladder. Sunlight shone in through the plastic sheets I'd put over the windows for winter.

Mr. Parshall got there last, puffing for breath, and pulled his daughter out of the quilt and slapped her, making red spots on her thighs. You couldn't tell yet, at almost three months, that she was pregnant under the T-shirt. I wanted to go to Nell and take her from her father. The officers stood quietly till Mr. Parshall remembered they were there, then he stood back from Nell and yelled at her: "You're not like that! If you're having this baby, you get married! Who is this McGee? Was it him, not Anthony? It wasn't some—businessman! Go back to that Ladro Brown, go back to him! He'll marry you! He was always going to! It was still that Anthony, wasn't it? You have to admit it was that Anthony!"

"It wasn't Anthony!" yelled Nell.

They stared at each other, and I heard the policeman say to the policewoman quietly, "Anne, you recognize that quilt? And remember the curved wall? And the stepladder in that picture—"

I heard her say she did, and then I knew what trouble I could be in. I tried to get Nell to look at me. When she did, I fixed my eyes on hers, to watch every sign of what she was thinking with each word I said, so I would say only enough for her to take in, word by word, slowly. I said, looking only at her, "Mr. Parshall, Nell and—I" —she was staring at me with her soft eyes, her head not tilted in its old puzzled way, and she knew what I was going to say—"want to get married—"

Obsequy

Last week a quaint bit of local advertising came in our mail, a flyer with a photo of big Ladro holding a pathetically small brown paper bag next to a scrawny kid with a huge plastic More-For-Less bag, Ladro with a put-on look of envy. "He's still working there," said Nell.

"You should take some of those coupons and venture into the world, Nell."

"By myself?"

I didn't like thinking of her sitting in all day now it was getting warm. She needed to do something. "You don't have to go to the shopping center. Start by going to the corner store."

"If I went to the shopping center I might see Ladro."

I didn't think that would be so bad. I was hoping Nell might work herself up to calling Ruthie, or Josie, some afternoon. "There's always the library," I said. "You could walk up there. Still have your card?"

A few mornings later, while I was finishing the eggs Nell had gotten up to fix for me before I went to work, she told me she had decided to go to the library, to see if she could do it. "I want to look if they ever got Anthony's books in the O's," she said.

When I came home at six, Nell was in her room with the door closed. She didn't answer when I called. She might be napping, I thought. In the bedroom, on what I was beginning to think of as our bed, though Nell still had her own bed as well, were two library books, the Soliloquy and the Colloquy, in heavy red library bindings almost as thick as the pages they enclosed. I lay down, admired them as I always did whenever I picked up anybody's copies of Anthony's books, and then began to read here and there.

There was Frank's pen-and-ink of the windswept heights, two tiny figures struggling across. " 'Why should this ever be over?' " said David to Jonathan on the facing page. " 'This will always go on.' 'Our struggle?' asked Jonathan. 'When it is over you'll have to weep for me,' he said. 'Never over, never over,' said David, struggling along in the wind."

I heard Nell's door open across the landing. I saw her, in her plaid robe, coming around to me. She had a third library book in her hand, its dust jacket protected in a plastic cover, and I soon saw it was the Letters.

"I did go out," said Nell.

"The library—"

"This was on the shelf too," she said in a flat voice. "I read it, Burt, all day."

"I didn't want you to see it," I said. "I didn't think of it being in the library."

"Do you have one?"

"I've kept it at work."

"Burt," she said, kneeling beside the bed, with her arm reaching along the blue quilt to me, "I never read a whole book before in a day."

"The last letters?"

She opened the book and read to me: "Where he says, 'I know she'll have the baby now, because I'm going to do something that will make her have the baby—' "

"We could understand that several ways," I said. "Maybe he

planned to steal you from your parents again, or talk to your
parents, get them to make you marry him, or—"

"I know what he meant," Nell said. "It's easy enough to know.
He was going to do something, by himself, to make me. And the
next letter he says, 'I don't think she'll keep the baby after it's
born. She'll want to forget everything about it. If you and Martin
could somehow get the baby, adopt it, take it away even, be its
parents if she won't, because she's too young still and she doesn't
know what it means.' "

"But it's so confused, Nell. He wants you to have the baby, and
then he's saying you're too young. He wrote those letters in his
panic, Nell. It wasn't the way he felt about you."

"He was right I didn't know what it means."

"Neither did he, of course," I said. I leaned on my side to touch
her arm, the three library books on the bed between us.

"And so he wanted to get hit by that bus, Burt?" She looked
up at me with an empty face, eyes wide open, lips apart.

"He was thinking his baby wouldn't be born," I said, "and
maybe he thought what was his life to its? In a panic he could
have thought that, maybe after too many beers—"

Nell sat up, getting mad. "He thought he knew all that and
what I'd do for certain? Who says I wouldn't have the abortion
still? How did he know what he'd make me do? How could he
say he loved the baby already, and go die for it when it wasn't
even born? How could he think he'd kill himself and it wouldn't
be worse than me having the abortion? What did he think he was
leaving me with?"

"I think of those last letters as what he thought only at
moments, in a panic," I said, "and he wrote to Elsa, letting
thoughts come out to her without thinking, because she was his
sister, he didn't have to control himself for her. That night it was
only in drunkenness, maybe, running helplessly, or even running
over here, to see me, for help, I don't know—"

"Elsa says he was sacrificing himself," Nell said.

"Those stupid bits by Elsa—to write that way of her own
brother's death—"

"And the way she says at the end that if N does go have the
baby, and if N wants it to have a good home—I don't like being

this N!" Nell picked the book of letters off the quilt and tossed it at the wall across the room. She started to laugh, and she bounced up beside me on the bed and said, "Mr. S!"

Kitchell knows how to avoid being taken to court. There's no description of the round house except as "Mr. S's house." No one can come looking for this N and me. I looked down at her, lying beside me, at her slight smile. "I'd thought the book would jolt you," I said.

"I thought I let Anthony die," Nell said, "but if partly he wanted to die himself—and even if he didn't want to, I didn't know he even thought of it, even once. I didn't know he thought he knew so much more than me. I thought he still loved me more than everything. I didn't know he thought I was so young. But he was young too, Burt. Like what you said, how he'll always be eighteen now, and we get older and older. I'm as old as him now. Soon I'll be older than him forever."

I held Nell close to me and felt suddenly tired, and she sounded sort of sleepy too. "In those letters he isn't the same Anthony, Burt. I only had my Anthony to be sad about, but he didn't love me as much as that all the time. When he died he was even hating me because I wouldn't do what he wanted. He said to Elsa why he liked to write was because that was the only time he could make everything the way he wanted. He said to her how he hated me for what I was going to do."

Nell had still been only seventeen and needed her parents' consent for us to marry last November. They gave it, because that was what they wanted, that she get married if she was going to have the baby. Mr. Parshall, on the sunny third floor of the round house, had said, "It wasn't the dead boy, then—it was you. Those tutoring sessions I paid you for—"

The policewoman and policeman had watched us carefully.

Nell started laughing at her father. "You don't know anything," she said. Mr. Parshall moved toward her again, but the policewoman was in his way.

"Mr. Parshall," I said, "perhaps it doesn't matter who it was. If you'll let me marry Nell, the baby and its mother will have a home. I don't know how it will go from there. No one knows that." He looked at me, up and down, considering me. "The clothes Liam left," I explained to the two police, "I gave them to Nell once when hers got wet coming over in the rain for tutoring."

"We have two separate situations after all," said the policewoman. "Gerry, why don't you take Mr. Parshall and his daughter home. It's not our business, unless he wants to make it be. Mr. Stokes, if you could get the girl's own clothes and then I'd like you to walk with me back to the station, if you don't mind, so we can talk further about the McGee boy."

Anne, the policewoman, wasn't unpleasant to me. It was almost a friendly talk we had that morning walking down to the avenue. "If you could see all the things I have to see," she said a couple of times, to let me know this was a small matter in her day.

At the station, she told me, frankly, that the pictures they had of Liam had certainly been taken in my house. I said Liam had been working for me, and he had a key, and he had used the house when I was away visiting my parents, and he could have taken the pictures then. She got them out of her desk. She wasn't embarrassed by them. As she passed them to me one by one, I realized I was holding them at the same angle, with the same hand that there in the last photograph was reaching toward the boy on the ladder. She didn't say anything but watched me closely.

"I don't intend to tell his parents about this additional wrinkle," she said. "They don't seem to care much about him anyway. But, Mr. Stokes, if you hear from that boy again, please let me know. And as for Nell Parshall, I shouldn't say it, but is it really the thing you should let yourself in for? Unless of course, the two of you love each other." With a polite smile and friendly handshake, she saw me to the door.

Mr. Parshall called that afternoon to say that on Monday he would go to the town hall to fill out the consent form. I should get my blood test and the license and make arrangements with a justice of the peace. He didn't want to see me again, and his wife didn't want to see me. Nell would be with her aunt for the week, and I could call her there. She could then collect her things from her old home, but once she'd moved out they didn't want to see her again. He said it in his tired voice, as if it all meant nothing to him.

I went to the shopping center, to More-For-Less's furniture basement, and ordered a bed for the empty room that would be Nell's. I kept an eye out to avoid Ladro in the hardware department. I still expected to bump into him someday, as I'd once told Nell I would, but with Anthony dead we wouldn't find ourselves joking about old times. What would he make of me marrying his Nell?

I reached back in the space in the dining-room wall where I'd hidden Nell's clothes and pulled out Liam's pictures again. I had looked at them often after he left town, but then not again since the night Anthony appeared at my door in tears. The pictures the police had were from the first set, which I didn't have. The set Liam gave me copies of had more than just my reaching hand in them, but the parts of me weren't identifiable as mine. It was Liam you looked at anyway. I decided I would have to tell Nell about Liam before we got married. I couldn't leave it as something for her to find out, somehow, later.

I waited on the town-hall steps one day after school. Nell's aunt drove into the parking lot to drop her off and drove right out. After we got the license, we went across to the sub shop to talk.

"I didn't know if this would be the right thing," I said.

"It was the right thing," said Nell. "It was the only thing."

"I thought you could tell what I was thinking when I looked at you with all of them there, your father, the police."

"You kept staring at me. I had an idea," Nell said.

"Does it make you feel strange?"

"Yes."

"It makes me feel very strange," I said. "It suddenly came to me. I wouldn't have thought of it five minutes earlier."

"I would never have thought of it," she said. "Burt—I have to say Burt now."

"Nell, this is what I want for you, that you have a quiet safe time to have the baby, that you and the baby have a home, and whatever happens afterwards, you can decide. It's for Anthony I want to do this, but it's for you too, and it should be most of all for the baby."

"It's for Anthony I want to do this too," she said.

"I don't expect anything from you."

"I know," she said.

In silence we began eating our subs. No one was there in that time between after-school snacks and supper. I didn't know how to begin about Liam.

"You might wonder about Liam," I said without thinking what I'd say next.

"He's gone."

"But that he was at my house so much."

"He won't be around now," Nell said. "It's all right."

"But if something of him came back to trouble us, to hurt you— I think it will be all right, but the police have pictures of him that were taken at my house. Did you hear them say they recognized that quilt? It was in those pictures. But I took the pictures for him. They were pictures he used—"

"When he went downtown, right?" said Nell. "I figured Liam would do things like that. He sure dressed like it."

"But I took the pictures for him," I said.

"It's all right, Mr. Stokes. It's all right, Burt, I mean."

"Can you imagine what the pictures were like?"

"I figure he doesn't have much clothes on."

"I wanted you to know I did something like that, before I had you marrying me, not knowing about it."

"It's all right, Burt," she said.

We ate slowly, quietly, and then I knew I had to say more. "I went to bed with him too," I said. "It all happened in a way I didn't expect."

"Anthony said Liam could always get people to do what he wanted," Nell said.

"But I wanted to do it too," I said, feeling I'd finally said it.

"It's all right, Burt. You think I don't know about things like that?"

"Maybe it'll make you feel safer getting married to me," I said.

"I always feel safe with you anyway," she said. "I don't know what else to do now. If I'm going to have the baby—"

"Have you thought about it again, that you want to?"

"Yes."

"For Anthony?"

"Yes."

"But for yourself too?"

"Yes."

"The last time to do anything else about it is passing."

"Yes," Nell said. After we'd eaten, I walked her over to the street where her aunt lived, but she asked me to leave her at the corner.

When we were married, I left the school and looked for a new job. I don't know how the news of Nell and me became known. Mrs. Parshall may have made the mistake of confiding in Mrs. McGee. Someone at the town hall may have known someone at the high school, someone's brother-in-law, someone in the same church. I wasn't asked to resign, but I think I would have been eventually. Enough kids knew about it. Isabel McGee said to me, after what turned out to have been my last class, "I hear you got married to that girl, Mr. Stokes? The girl that went with Anthony Ogna Santy? You really got married?" I smiled and shuffled papers on my desk. "If Liam calls, I'll tell him," she said. "He won't believe it Mr. Stokes married a high school kid."

Nell was afraid for me, that I wouldn't find another job, that I'd given up my job for her, and she did worry that the police would come by again about Liam. But I told her we were safe and, once I got my new job, how much I liked it, how glad I was to be away from teaching for a while. "Someday maybe I'll look for another teaching job, where none of this matters, in some better school."

"But we won't leave the round house," she said, worried. "I want to just stay here."

"I'll commute."

"Still, everything could change someday," she said. "Burt, if I didn't have you, I'd be in some home for unwed mothers. Saint Ursula's runs something like that." She shivered, and so I reached down from the big chair to rub her shoulders while she sat on the rug before the fire. "Burt, you gave everything you had to me, all at once, everything you had. What did you leave for you?"

Paula and Frank had been entirely surprised by what had happened. I waited to write a letter till after Nell had moved in and after I had the new job. Then Paula called me at work, where I couldn't really talk to her, so I called her from home that night, and after a long talk, full of her worries, her doubts, she asked me to put Nell on.

I heard what Nell said: "Hello, Mrs. Innocenzo ... I feel all right ... No, it's nice here ... No, they won't see me ... Ruthie? No, I don't see her. We're not really friends anymore. I don't see anyone. My aunt calls sometimes ... Yeah, Burt made me a nice room ... A separate one for the baby ... May ... Anthony, or Antonia ... I will ... He is ... He really is ... Yeah, good-bye."

Paula and Frank sent us a wedding present, from Frank's rare books, two old leather-bound volumes, Romeo and Juliet and the Inferno in Italian. Nell looked through them at the engravings. She wanted to keep them beside her bed. Later Paula sent something more practical, a white blanket she'd knitted for the baby. Frank wanted me to send my Xerox of the complete Obloquy, because he was serious about making a whole book of it, if Kitchell didn't get it first. I didn't know what was involved legally, if Elsa had the manuscript or who had rights to it.

One evening I came down to answer the bell and there stood Brother Nor on the front step in his parka, December's first light snow falling behind him. He had a small package under his arm. I made him some tea, and we sat at the kitchen table.

"I should've come earlier," he said, "or called, but Brother Don was out and I couldn't leave the boys, and then I thought I should check if your lights were still on. It was a pleasant walk over in this snow."

"I'm always up late," I said, "now that I don't have to get up so early."

"You're working where now?"

"It's a reinsurance firm. Mostly paper work. It's nothing I enjoy, but after eleven years of kids all day, I find it relaxing, that matter-of-factness. Well, if anyone knows about kids all day, it's you," I said.

"There are moments my soul yearns for a hermitage," said Brother Nor.

"Silence, a little cell somewhere—" I said, smiling with him. "I used to be somewhat of a monk myself."

"And now you're married?" I hadn't thought to wonder if he knew. Nell was in her room upstairs, asleep, or watching TV.

The surprise of finding Brother Nor at my door had, for a moment, made me forget she was there. "It's not for me to say, Mr. Stokes, of course, but I do think you've done something very kind. Monsignor thought so too when he heard of it. If you'd ever like to talk to him, he would be glad. He feels he could perhaps help Nell too, and of course there's the baby soon to think of. There was a lot I didn't know about Anthony's last days, I now see. I've had a bit of a time meditating on it all. His books help me. I've read them all many times. Which brings me to this—" He reached for the package he'd set on the stool beside him when he took his parka off. He untied the string and, unfolding the crinkled brown paper, he said, "Of course, Mr. Kitchell has the manuscripts of the first two for safe-keeping, or perhaps he's sent them on to Elsa, but this Obloquy manuscript was in Anthony's room when Miss Burnham cleaned it out and brought me everything. And then to my surprise, there was this as well."

Below the first notebook was another one. Obsequy it said on the cover, and the name Antonio Ognissanti, and at the bottom: In Memory of Elsa Ognissanti 1900–1980. I turned to the first page. It began: "Memory? I never saw her, I will never see her, I always see her." I looked up at Brother Nor.

"A fourth book," he said, "that I knew nothing of."

"Anthony told me he was writing something new, but in those last weeks, in his panic—"

"Miss Burnham said he worked every day. He kept asking her for more used paper."

"And those drafts?"

"She said they weren't in his room, no library books either, which surprised her because he took out so many, and none of the paper she'd given him, only these two tidy notebooks. It occurred to Monsignor that Anthony might have burned his first drafts in the incinerator at the church. Anthony was still doing custodial work there, once a week."

"But if he burned everything, if he returned all the library books—"

Brother Nor looked across at me sadly. "It makes us think he knew he would find a way to die, doesn't it, Mr. Stokes."

I said it did.

"No," he said, "how I hope not! I've read and I've read those books. I've felt somewhat like a detective, or psychologist, or—well, I have to come back to the fact that I'm a religious man and that I'm looking for the spirit of things. Please, Mr. Stokes, read them again, read this last new one, this Obsequy, and look for the spirit of it. Is it written by a boy planning to kill himself? How much I don't think so! How much I feel it's the work of a young artist, who is learning to control, who will not relinquish this control he's learned—he's aching to make this work right, and to grow, and go on to the next and make it right, and the next. Not a dying boy, Mr. Stokes!"

"I'll read it tonight. I won't sleep till I read it," I said.

"And then call me, as a man of letters—"

"I?"

"Yes, and as his teacher—" Brother Nor's eyes were close to brimming with tears again. "I think he burned the papers," he said, "to make his next start fresh. He always burned his drafts. Why have old notes of old books, old variants and false starts to shadow the clarity of the finished work?"

"But returning the library books—"

"Perhaps he was going away and he knew he wouldn't have another chance to return them. Monsignor was visiting at a school in the country that week, you know. He told Anthony, when Anthony came to tell him everything, that he would inquire about a place for him at that school, tutoring younger boys, to let Anthony leave this town for a while, be of help to those who were lost, as he had once been lost. Monsignor felt Anthony might do that. And I think he returned the books because he'd decided he would be going to that school."

I nodded and nodded, thinking how unlikely it seemed. I asked what he planned to do with the notebooks.

"I sent a big package to Elsa, his own copies of his books, all his other belongings, his clothes, his camera, his watch that still worked even after the accident, the poster on his door, whatever else. But I had to read these books first myself. I couldn't let them go. I told her a lie, Mr. Stokes. I answered a letter of hers, a rather odd letter, I might say, and said that I believed his last work was with the man in Providence who had published those three fragments. So I thought I could give the Obloquy manuscript to you, and you could give it to Mr. Innocenzo, and he could deal with it. But then this Obsequy, well, I don't think anyone knows of it but you and me. I thought I should give it to, well, if I may—" I knew he would give it to me, and I smiled across at him. "—to your young wife. And someday, of course, to his child."

"Where it should be," I said taking the little notebook. Why didn't it feel as much of a treasure as that first copy of the Soliloquy I brought to Anthony that night in the light rain? "I'll read it tonight, Brother Nor, and then Nell and I will read it together, the way we did the Soliloquy, back when I was tutoring her, and the Colloquy later on, and the Obloquy we're just finishing now from the Xerox."

"How stupid of me, I meant to bring you something else, Mr. Stokes," Brother Nor said, slapping his forehead. He seemed cheerier now. "There was a little card with some lines in French taped by Anthony's desk. Miss Burnham gave me that too. It was a strange thought, if I understood it correctly. I'll send it to you if you'd like to have it."

"I would, Brother Nor," I said, thinking Anthony was more part of my dream than I was of his.

The next day I mailed the Obloquy notebook to Frank, to make Brother Nor's lie into the truth, and in the next evening, Nell and I settled in by the fire, both of us squeezed together in the big chair, to read the Obsequy. She had looked the title up in my Webster's. "It comes from follow toward," she said. "Anthony always told me to not just read what the word means. He said to read the part that says where it comes from."

The Obsequy made me think of the Dinesen tales he was reading on my recommendation, or a story like Kafka's Josephine the Singer—perhaps even something out of the tales of Poe, or Hoffmann. Had I made Anthony's imagination more Gothic than it might otherwise have been with those reading lists of mine?

Embedded in his meditation on the possibility of remembering what you never knew, there was a fable, told not in the fragmentary phrases of the Obloquy but in ramblingly long whole sentences. Anthony was trying something new. He described an Italian palace, which resembled, I noticed, our town's library, gray brick, a great hall with a gallery around it. There was a gathering of nobility. Every year they came there, seated about the hall, expectant, on the edges of their straight-backed chairs, glancing at each other and then always back to the curtained door at the end of the hall. The music master, Umbertocchini, finally appeared from a little side door and announced, to everyone's disappointment, that he had once again failed to engage la Clara, the brilliant young singer they had all come to hear, whom all of them remembered from years ago—how many years was it they had been returning to the hall of the Count and Countess d'Innocenzo in hope of hearing again that ever-young Clara? But Umbertocchini, as always, has brought other promising young artists to entertain the guests, and as he presents them, one by one, we fall into his thoughts, and his regrets. He knows la Clara is gone, but it is only in hope of hearing her that his audiences come back. They would not bother for these others, pleasing as their music is. Umbertocchini falls asleep in his chair by the little side door, and the Countess, through her lorgnette, peers at him disapprovingly from her thronelike chair in the center of the hall, the Count beside her. And then the narrative switches to a young man on a narrow balcony in moonlight. In the distance a Brindisi is being sung in a light, thin voice, nothing like la Clara's. The young man tells us that the Count and Countess once had a daughter, who sang songs to herself in the palace gardens where she played, but she had a disease of the lungs and as she grew she was seen less frequently, and at last it was thought she had died. Could it be, the young man wonders, that her parents kept her alive, tutored by Umbertocchini, and at last as a young woman she sang that single time, a voice nurtured for one perfect performance before its breath gave out?

Nell loved it because it was the nearest to a regular story Anthony had written, and she knew how to follow a story like that. It didn't puzzle her the way his other books had, but it did puzzle me. Brother Nor looked in it for hope, but Umbertocchini seemed such a character of no hope. He slept, kept sleeping through the rest of the Obsequy, as if it were his dream. My only comfort for Brother Nor, when I called him the morning after his visit, was that in order to have the Obsequy in fair copy, Anthony must have completed it sometime before the last few days of his life. "And I know, Brother Nor," I said, "that he still hoped, even on the night he snuck Nell out her window and brought her here—he hoped to have me hide her, keep her safe for him. The Obsequy must tell only his fears of losing what he loved, Brother Nor, not any certain course of doom."

"Thank you, Mr. Stokes. I think so too. And I think it also tells of a promise, that expectant audience, that curtained door. They keep coming every year to the palace of the Innocenzi."

I don't know if Brother Nor has seen Elsa's book. How would he interpret the last letters? How would he read the line about Anthony doing something to make Nell have the baby? Will he call me if he reads the book, ask for my reassurance again, as his man of letters?

I haven't heard from him since I called to postpone further our Antonia's baptism. Paula and Frank were going to be godparents, the Monsignor was to have performed the ceremony. I had to lie terribly: Brother Nor knew the doubts we had already expressed, that we had to follow our own feelings, that neither Nell nor I felt ourselves part of the church, that while Anthony would have wanted it we still had to take our own responsibility as parents, that I could not live out my life as a deputy for a dead boy, that if Antonia was our child we could only give her what religion we felt we had. Brother Nor understood me. He told me the church would always be there. "And to you, Mr. Stokes," he said, "who are taking on the care of a human life you never created, I can say it can be as great a joy as actual parenthood."

He and the Monsignor still do not know that Antonia has been taken. No one knows, not even Paula and Frank, who will have to be told soon. Paula was here to help out right after Nell came home from the hospital, and she intends to take the bus up to see us again at the end of the summer.

The third night Nell was in the hospital and I was home alone, thinking of the baby girl that was mine now, the crib that waited for her, the white blanket Paula had knitted, the supply of diapers, the doorbell rang, and I ran down, happy as I'd ever been, wondering why Paula had come up a day early. I opened the door to Liam.

"I been at my grandmother's," he said. "I saw your light up the hill from her window."

"I'm a father," I said, not even thinking what I was saying. He looked at me as if I was crazy. He came in past me and into the center hall. "Liam," I said, "where did you go all these months? All that's happened since—"

He slipped his leather jacket off his skinny shoulders and tossed it on the floor. He looked very thin. I could see scratches on his pale arms. I felt an ache in me. "I thought you went where there was sun all winter," I said.

"I been all over," he said. "She here?"

"Nell? She just had her baby. She's at the hospital."

"She living here with you?"

"Yes."

"So Mrs. Constantine still lets you stay here." He started up the stairs, running his hand along the polished bannister. "I want to look what you did to this place," he said.

"Not much since you left." I came up to the top of the first flight and watched him walk around the landing, looking in the doors. He went on to the third floor, but I stood and waited, almost scared. "I haven't done anything up there," I said, "just moved my desk up."

He came back down again and walked into my room, and then I followed him. "The quilt," he said, smiling at it. I'd been on the bed reading when he rang the bell. The lamp was shining bright over the pillows, the rest of the room in shadow. "See this," he said, pulling up his T-shirt and turning toward the light to show me his back. It had three thin red marks across it, as if from a whip. He pulled his shirt down, turned, and looked at me.

"Are you all right, Liam?"

"Sometimes I'm all right, sometimes I'm not," he said.

"Do you want something to eat? Let's go downstairs—I'll make you something."

He followed me down to the kitchen. While I got out bowls and mugs, he opened the icebox and stared into it.

I didn't know how to talk to him. "You're at your grand-mother's?" I asked, wanting to talk about everything else.

"I told her not to tell my parents. She won't tell them. She hates them too. They put her off in that box. She's sort of crazy, though. She doesn't know what time it is."

"How about some stew?"

"I want to eat in the dining room," he said. "I never ate in there. I did all those moldings and those drawers."

I heated up a can of stew, warmed some bread, filled his mug with milk because he didn't want beer. We took it all into the dining room, a room I never use, and he sat at the far end of the table from me.

"I know all what you been doing," he said. "My sisters told me. I call collect when my parents are out, bowling nights, church-group nights. My parents think I'm an electrician in Texas. They get these bills with Houston, Austin, other places. My sisters think it's funny about you and Nell."

"Are you going to stay at your grandmother's?"

"Not for long, man."

"Liam, do you know about the police arresting that guy you made the pictures for, and your pictures being at the police station? They showed them to your parents. They showed them to me."

"What's the big deal?" he said.

"They want me to let them know if I ever hear from you."

"You won't tell anyone," he said. "I won't tell anyone about you." He didn't look at me as he ate the stew. Crumbs from his bread were spreading on the table around his bowl.

"What've you been doing, Liam? You're so skinny, and your back—"

"I meet some weird people," he said.

"I missed you," I said suddenly.

He looked down the table at me. His skin was a little rough, his hair tangled and dirty and longer than before, and he looked older. I could see scratches on his forearms as he held his mug of milk to his lips.

"I'll tell you something I did once you didn't know," he said. "Last spring, some afternoon, I came to find you at school."

"When?"

"That guy with the pictures told me he thought they were on to him. He was nice. He told me he tore out the page where he had the number where people called me sometimes here. I was scared though. I didn't know if they'd try to get me and send me somewhere. I was scared that day he told me. So I go to your classroom after school's out, I'm too scared to even wait, and there's Anthony in there with you. I didn't want to see him in there. So then I figure I can wait till you get home, it isn't that bad. I went over to the sub shop."

"I remember," I said. "I thought it was Ladro. You disappeared down the hall."

"Then I didn't tell you later about it. I kept thinking about you and Anthony, and then I didn't want to tell you about the guy maybe getting me in trouble. But where did I have to go nights anymore? I got along for a while, with some different people, but then I had to get out of here to somewhere else. You didn't want me still around all summer again with Anthony being Mr. Shakespeare."

"Your sisters have told you what happened—"

"What do you think!" I looked at him, to see if it made him sad at all, under his tight stare. "You think I came back here because there's no Anthony?"

"No."

"I didn't come back for you. I felt like seeing my sisters, my grandmother. I'm not staying for long." The corner of his lip curled, and he almost laughed. "You're married anyway, man."

"I wasn't suggesting anything, Liam. I want to know how you feel."

"You make me feel bad," he said, still staring.

"Why?"

"You always make me feel bad."

"Why?"

"You and Mrs. Innocenzo and all them."

"What does she have to do with it anymore?"

"Everybody here makes me feel bad."

"Your sisters?"

"I saw them this afternoon. That was enough. What do they know!"

He scraped at the sides of his bowl for bits of stew. I drank my beer, remembering how he always only talked about himself, how boring he got to be, but still I began to feel sad about him.

"Would you like to hear about Anthony's daughter?" I asked.

"No."

"About Nell and how we ended up married?"

"You want an award, man?"

"Liam, you don't think about anyone. You never—"

"Shut up. I could tell the police about you and those pictures." His lip curled again, and he sat back in the chair and stretched his pale arms.

"You're all scratched," I said.

"Sometimes I get treated rough."

"Aren't you scared of that?"

"I'm always scared. That's how I am, Burt. Would you like that?"

"Can't you find some sunny place, some kinder people?"

"You tell me where."

"You think I don't worry about you?" I said. "You think I'm just scared you'll tell the police? But you were over eighteen—what could happen, an embarrassing hearing, maybe? Liam, I worry about you, not because I'm scared of you—"

"You could take me to the third floor and tie me onto that ladder and do things," he said with a hard look at me.

"Liam, stop," I said.

"What did you ever do, man? It was something like that all along."

"It wasn't."

"Yes, it was, man."

"Liam—"

"Why didn't you do something else? You were supposed to be my teacher. You were my teacher, man. Why didn't you do something?"

"Liam—"

"Now that you got a baby, you think you're a real kind person. I didn't know she was born yet—I wouldn't've come here then. I just came into town on a bus. I went to my grandmother's and listened to her yap for a while. I went and saw my sisters after school. I thought I'd come here and find you and that Nell and tell her something she might like to know."

"I didn't marry her until she knew about you and me, Liam."

"Maybe I'd tell her about Anthony and me."

"What would that do?"

"You think Anthony's so perfect."

"Liam," I said, trying to think hard what was in his mind, "it's you who keeps thinking Anthony's so perfect. You remember him from when you wanted to save him, adopt him. He's always been with you that way."

"He scratched me and bit me and told me to stay away from him forever."

"He was scared of you, Liam."

"Why does everyone always be scared?"

"You too," I said, "you said so."

"You too, man," he said.

"Scared of someone controlling you—"

"That's right!" said Liam. He pushed his chair back, stood and walked to the window where he looked out at the lights in the far tall buildings. "I went around that old block when I got in on the bus," he said. "It was the same there. That Midnite Books place I used to go, I think it bought that Spondee place. It's all one place now. There were still people hanging around. I talked to a guy who said he knew Anthony, some publisher guy. Maybe I'll go down there tonight and see what I can get."

"You could stay here," I said, not thinking.

"When's she coming from the hospital?"

"Tomorrow. Paula's coming from Providence to help."

"So I can spend the night and get out before Mrs. Innocenzo comes."

"What can I do, Liam?"

"I want those pictures I gave you," he said.

"The copies you gave me?"

"Those were the only ones. I just said they were copies. They were for you."

I glanced at the drawers in the wall. "I burned them because of Nell," I said.

"I wanted to sell them, make some money," Liam said. "I need some money."

"You want to stay here tonight?"

"Why should I stay with you?"

"Only if you want to."

"You said you missed me," he said.

"I do." I imagined myself going and picking him up in my arms.

"What do you miss?" He walked over and put his hands on my shoulders. I could feel his stomach against the back of my head. "You won't miss me now," he said. "You have a baby and some girl to be your wife."

"You don't say fuck anymore, Liam," I said, leaning back into his stomach.

"Why should I say it?" I pulled his hands around and kissed them, on the scratches, kissed them where the veins were on his wrists. "You won't miss me anymore," he said.

"What are you going to do? There's nothing anywhere for you to do, Liam."

"You won't tell the police I was here?" he asked.

"Of course not."

"Maybe you'll be a good father." He walked into the center hall and picked up his jacket from the floor. As he stuck his arms into it, I came and reached under his T-shirt and felt the red marks.

"No—" he said.

"Does it hurt?"

"No."

"If you'd write me, or call, and tell me where you are when you disappear—"

"I won't come back," he said and walked to the door and out it.

As soon as he'd gone, I tried to stop thinking about him. I tried to tell myself I wouldn't miss him anymore, having seen him and remembered how he could be. Nell, although she'd spent her pregnancy about the house, just watching TV and sleeping, although she'd never been happy since she got pregnant, still had managed to give me a new life. I went back to thinking about our baby.

Nell hadn't expected me to take as much care of her as I had, but she had let me. She had come shopping with me sometimes, and out to dinner and a movie, but except for visits to the doctor, she had spoken to no one but me, and to Paula and Frank when they had come to see us New Year's Day. Paula had been very curious about how Nell felt being pregnant. She took her off and talked with her alone while Frank caught me up on his business.

The Obloquy was set for publication in July, the first in a series of Trochee books. Frank was certain Kitchell had no rights to it, and he'd brave him in court if it came to that. "But he's got his pal Sarah working on it," Frank said, pulling out of his jacket a copy of that month's Iambus—A Review Of The Arts, folded open to an article on Ognissanti, in which Sarah Bowen analysed and praised his two books (available from the Spondee Press, she noted) and pled for the release of the third, known as yet only from fragments in a small (unnamed) magazine. To my surprise, she mentioned a fourth book as well, written just before his death and referred to, she revealed, in his last letters to his sister. Where was it? It was not among his effects. Had it existed only in destroyed drafts? The article had a fearful tone, as if there were forces conspiring to keep Ognissanti's last works from appearing. Spondee, she was pleased to say, was doing what it could to obtain the third manuscript and search for the fourth and, in the meantime, was planning to issue those letters to his sister sometime in May, organizing them in sections that corresponded to his four books. The last "Obsequy letters" were a testament of hope and despair, according to Sarah Bowen, careful to leave both interpretations open. "I met him at that time," she wrote, "at a gathering of writers and artists. He had a fiery face, still a child's, but with a wildness behind the eyes that terrified me. Returning home in early morning, a group of us, I watched him ride standing, in the back of our van, letting the turns of the road sway him. He would stumble, leap up again, swaying before us all. No one touched him or helped him balance, and he spoke to none of us."

"What a crock, eh?" said Frank.

"I have that fourth book, Frank," I said. "Nell has it. Brother Nor's the only person who knows we have it."

Frank reached across the table and grasped both my hands with his bigger ones, shook them triumphantly, smiling wide between beard and mustache. He spent the rest of the afternoon on the couch reading the Obsequy, while Nell and Paula talked upstairs and I got supper for everyone. When they left, Frank was already planning a November publication, the next open slot in the Trochee's series. "I was thinking I'd do a set of photographs, architectural details of the town library," he said. "The Innocenzo palace, it seems to me, is modeled on the closest thing in our town to the Italian renaissance."

"Frank does nothing but photography now," said Paula. She promised she would come up again when she could, but if she couldn't make it before the birth, she'd definitely come afterwards, to help out. "Not that I know anything about babies," she said as she kissed us good-bye.

When Nell read the Letters, a week ago now, it set me thinking again about my idea of writing to Elsa. A photograph of Antonia, for my desk at work, a word of how she is—would Elsa be willing to send us that much? So I wrote her, taking the address from the envelope of her warning letter. My letter was short, as polite and impersonal as I could make it. Nell told me not to expect any response at all.

Nell has been out two more times this past week, once down to shop along the avenue, once, on a hot day, to the air-conditioned shopping center. She told me she saw Ruthie in the shoe store and they went to eat at the lunch place where Nell used to work. She didn't tell me much about their talk, just that it had been Josie, as she'd suspected, who'd thought she was pregnant, but it turned out she wasn't. Josie had slept with Ladro once but mostly with some other boys. Nell didn't seem excited about being back in touch with Ruthie. It was as if she'd seen her all along, she said, as if they'd never drifted apart. "Funny thinking about Ladro going with Josie," she said. "He used to call her Six-Pack because it takes you a six-pack before she starts looking good to you."

"What did you tell Ruthie about your baby?" I asked, across the big bed to where Nell was sitting on the edge.

"She heard all the rumors, even how we gave the baby up for adoption. That's what I told her happened."

"Nell, are you feeling a little numb out in the world again?"

"Maybe," she said with a yawn. "I don't feel like sleeping in here tonight, Burt. Some nights I don't. I don't know why. I'll go watch TV. Do you mind, Burt?"

Of course I didn't mind, I told her.

I lay on top of the sheets with a summer breeze blowing in on me. I hoped for a picture of Antonia. I thought of how her dark hair had begun to fall out, how her little eyes were darkening. I thought of Nell in her robe, walking along the second-floor landing with the white package of the baby in her arms, walking back and forth till Antonia slept. I remembered wondering after Elsa's warning letter if Martin had come east, if he'd come try to convince us to let them adopt our girl and take her back to Oregon to Elsa. I had decided I would be calm if he came, polite, understanding, kind. I knew I could show him how all was well with the three of us here, and he might even reassure us, say Elsa was strange at times but he was taking her to a doctor and someday perhaps she'd understand and the two of them could come see their niece, or send her presents.

On Antonia's last night with us, we had both put her to bed. Nell had stood by her crib humming after I'd watched the little eyes close. And then we'd gone to our separate rooms, Nell to fall asleep with the TV, I to read. It was not my usual late night, since we'd both been up the night before each time Antonia cried. All our lights were out soon, except the TV's glow under Nell's door across the hall. I barely heard its noise.

Later I thought I heard Nell going in to check the baby, but I turned over and was back asleep for a minute. Some sort of noise must have waked me again. I heard light steps on the stairs. From my bed I looked across the landing and saw the strip of blue light under Nell's door. It took me a moment to wonder why her door was still closed.

Half asleep I slipped out of bed and stood in my underwear on the landing. Then I leaned over the railing and thought I saw a

figure about to cross the hall downstairs. "Nell?" I said. I heard
nothing but the TV's buzz as I passed her door. I started down
the stairs, keeping my eye on the hall, dimly lit from the moon in
the skylight. The figure must have been slinking along the wall
under the stairs and ducked into the living room. I went first to
the front door, which was shut, then I heard a window open. I
ran to the living room. A shape crouched in the open window
behind the couch, something lumpy on its back. It was lowering
itself out the window, then it hung by its hands, then fell. I
leaped onto the couch and looked out and saw moonlight on a
leather jacket and the white papoose. I ran to the front door, ran
out in my underwear to the sidewalk, around the corner. I saw
nothing moving. I ran back to the house, along the side of it,
around it and around it again the other way. I saw nothing. I ran
back in and yelled to Nell. I ran upstairs, flipping each light
switch on as I passed. I ran into Antonia's room, and she was
gone. I ran into Nell's room, only able to say "Nell! Nell!" and
pull her out of bed to the next room. "Now, just now," I said,
"what I heard—I saw—"

"Where is she, Burt!"

"Get dressed." I ran to get dressed myself. I was quicker with
my overalls. Downstairs I opened the front door, and with all the
lights on, a key shone gold in the lock. Nell came running down
the stairs. "It's the extra one I gave Liam," I said. "It's not the
duplicate we had made for you."

"Liam?"

I ran onto the street, started running back and forth. Nell ran
one way around the block. After minutes of running, gasping, I
saw her running a block down and ran down to her. Her face
was covered with tears and she was raising her hands up and
down fast in front of her. I said, "Nell, Nell, Nell," and held her,
her arms around me, hands still going, as if trying to get rid of
something.

"The police—" I said.

"No!" she said with a gasping in of breath.

"But the police—"

She pushed away from me and ran back up toward the house,
all lighted on the hillside. That open window—

She had run to Antonia's room. I slammed the front door behind me and ran up to her. She stood at the crib, squeezing the headboard with white knuckles, staring at the blanket.

I pulled her into my arms and carried her to the bed, turned off the buzzing TV, and sat down by her side watching her breathe in gasps. I touched her cold face. We didn't say anything until finally she said, "I won't leave the round house, Burt."

"This is your home," I said.

"I won't go out, Burt, ever. I won't see anyone."

"I'll call the police. I'll deal with them."

"No," she said, looking at me as if she couldn't speak now.

"But if Martin was waiting for Liam with a car—" I felt I would get up and go to call the police any moment, but Nell's tears were coming again. She lay still, head back on the pillow, the tears running from the corners of her eyes down to fall in her ears. I thought she tried to say Liam, but she gulped and lay still again.

"It must be he's doing it for his old pal Elsa, for his old baby-sitter, who used to scrub his damn bottom!" I said. "When you were in the hospital he was here, Nell. I didn't tell you. He came and went, mad as hell at me. His damn leather jacket, I saw it out the window. He said he thought I'd be a good father! He had it planned then. He went around the house to see where everything was. He said he'd been hanging around that Midnite Books. I bet Martin was there seeing Kitchell about the letters, I mean about the books, Anthony's books, getting royalties or something. Or Liam called Elsa out in Oregon since he loves making collect calls. It could've even been his idea, just what crazy Elsa wanted to hear. But what if Martin was waiting with a car, around the corner, and by the time I ran out—The police can find them if he rented a car—"

Nell tensed her body and leaped off the bed and ran into Antonia's room. I went after her. "She's not there, Nell. Liam had the papoose on his back. She's gone."

"No!" Nell screamed, pounding on the headboard of Antonia's crib. She flung the blanket in the air, then the plastic-covered mattress. She fell on her knees and almost crawled under the crib, feeling all over the bare floor.

I knelt beside her, put my arm over her back, tried to pull her to me, to sit her up. Her arms were swinging around, even hitting me, until I reached all around her and held them at her side. Now she really sobbed and held me, pressed her face on the bib of my overalls, rubbing her wet cheek over to the bare skin of my side. I held her as tight as I could. And then I even looked up into the crib myself where there was no baby.

This is where I began the story: Our baby has been taken. We are alone in our empty house. Nell is out of her mind not knowing what to do. She trembles. She doesn't say a thing more. She has stopped listening.

In the weeks I've been here at work writing on this word processor, my panic leaving me, our panic, our loss, but my uncertain careful love for Nell with me still, and hers for me, I try to understand why I didn't call the police that night, and didn't the next morning either. All night I leaned against the wall in Antonia's room, holding Nell, and she did sleep, but I didn't. The light began to come in around the edges of the shade.

Just before one of her periods of silence, maybe a week later, I asked her, "Why didn't I get you from your locked room and bring you to the funeral? Why didn't I stay at school and let them try to fire me? Why don't I just go to the police now without you?"

"I don't know."

"Anthony wouldn't think of guilt or shame," I said.

"Anthony's baby's with his sister," Nell said. "Maybe he'd be glad." She was walking up the stairs in her robe with me behind her. She walked along the half circle of the landing, holding her own waist, and started up to the third floor.

"Come down, Nell," I said.

"I promise you I won't kill myself," she said, in the flat tone I was getting used to. She stood at the top, thin fingers on the bannister, all in light from above.

"Come down, Nell, I'll make supper." I started down, and I heard her on the stairs above me coming down, one step with each slow step of mine.

Every day was like that. At first I was afraid to leave her, so I took some sick days. I did nothing about any of the thoughts I had. When I called Brother Nor it was only to lie to him about the baptism, not to ask for help. I thought of calling the Monsignor, or a priest from Saint Ursula's, to come see Nell. I thought of calling the counselor at the hospital. I didn't call Paula.

As I sat up in bed each night after she slept, I tried to think how her life had been: that mother who went through her drawers looking for Tampax, that dead-tired father, the years with Ladro telling her what to do, and then Anthony—she fell in love with him through the thing that was hardest for her, through reading—and how scared she was of Ladro, though she thought she loved him still, but now that she loved Anthony—and feeling each other under the table in the O's, and making love in that little room in his rooming house, until the condom broke—then in her loneliness of not being able to talk to anyone, not to me, no longer to him, how it was to be back at school and pregnant, scared each day, and for her mother to find her out, and her father to lock her in, no one to help, till Anthony leads her along the slippery roof—and jumping off the back porch, and running, but to find him still wanting the same of her, to have the baby, and for him to hit at her as she left—how it was for her sneaking back into her house, in a basement window, up the stairs scared her parents would wake up, out onto the porch, along the roof, back in the window, in Liam's clothes, to have told her parents she would have the abortion and still to have them lock her in, to have them show her the newspaper that said the boy she loved was dead, hit by a bus—then to know, suddenly, she would keep the baby no matter what, to scream it at them and be dragged to the hospital as the boy is buried, made to scream her way out of an abortion, dragged home, beaten I'm sure, more than locked in—nailed in—fearing they'd force her, until a night the sirens go by and she smashes herself out to me—a lonely girl in all her socks and skirts and blouses running for help, and I listen and feed her and cover her, and tell her what she still has to hear about Anthony—to sleep an exhausted long sleep and then, hardly awake, running again, crouching in fear on my third floor, finally staring into the eyes of her teacher, her tutor, who is saying he will marry her—thrown out of her family, not seeing her friends, pregnant through a cold winter, cuddled by the fire reading

Anthony's last story, thinking each day she had let him die—a fatherly unknown husband reading with her, bringing her soup—an easy anaesthetized birth, spring coming, a sunny day, the baby on her blanket on the floor in the sunlight, what her own mother had never done, just to stare at her—and then at night, the theft, and running in the streets, and that weird boy's key in the lock, the open door, the moonlit silence, her feet running once again—

I want to understand her No. She tensed up in bed and ran to the empty crib. And later, a hundred times up and down the stairs, holding her stomach, or standing at the bannister squeezing the rail, or squeezing the crib's headboard, or shaking empty hands before her— Could she keep running looking for her child, and if she did not find her—

Her No said to let hope die. I never had to say a No. I only did nothing, nothing to make her risk another hope. This is all I can discover in me: that if I had called that policewoman, if I had told her what Liam had done, or even if I just said our baby had somehow been stolen for Elsa, and if Elsa was the one to name Liam McGee, but if they found him and brought him back, then after we got through the small shames of a trial, and Antonia was home and we began again, Liam would be sent away somewhere, at his age probably to jail for kidnapping. In me I must have begun to feel I'd never taken any care of him. Once I even found myself hoping Martin had paid Liam well for what he'd done, hoping Liam had come out of it with something. And so I didn't call the policewoman.

Yesterday—a photograph in the mail: Already? But I only just wrote to ask for it. Nell said not to expect anything at all. She's out all day, hasn't seen the mail. I'm opening it. No letter. A snapshot! Our older Antonia, two months old, propped up, smiling at a hand reaching from the camera toward her, a bare mattress beneath her, a pillow without a cover. Liam's hand, by its scratches. The postmark? Chicago. Still on his way to Oregon? What had he arranged with Martin? Our baby on a mattress in Chicago? Did Elsa tell him to send us a picture from his hiding place? I can't show it to Nell. What would it do to her to see that little face, black hair growing back, not to know why she's there, what she's smiling at—

And in the middle of this, Paula is pregnant. How can I even think of it now? She called last night from their summer artist commune, sniffling, happy. Frank was shouting in the background, "The count was low, but determined!" Nell talked to Paula, pretending Antonia was fine. Now that Paula was pregnant, I thought, we might be able to use the line that we'd given Antonia up for adoption. We hadn't wanted to before, with Paula so worried about her own childlessness. I began to think of a letter I could write her. On the phone Nell tried to tell Paula how she would be feeling as each month passed. I could see in Nell's eyes how hard it was to sound cheerful, and I remembered that envelope from Chicago in my pocket. What should I do?

Here I am at work, hardly doing a useful thing. What did Faye think, watching me this afternoon across the aisle? And now with the office to myself, the screen lit in front of me, I watch word by word appear as I type. I've caught up with my beginning. What should I do? Shuffle it into chronological order, a way it would make better sense than as it has come from my pulsing forehead? It's what these processors do: you push buttons and whole paragraphs, whole scenes move, silently, seamlessly. I believe Martin Keeney's business is servicing these things.

I take out the snapshot again. I'll put it on my desk, take the old one home. I look carefully at Liam's blurry arm as it grades into focus at the hand. Nothing follows.

A week.

This letter:

Dear Mr. Stokes,

I am writing for Elsa and myself. What does your letter mean, that you don't have the baby? Where is she, you're asking us? You mean she's actually gone? Elsa said she was writing you a letter a while back, but Elsa's had a hard time recently, Mr. Stokes. I don't think writing her book about her brother was the best thing for her, and for her to think his baby was being born when she can't have one. Elsa goes up and down ever since her parents died. You can imagine it's not the best time for both of us. But have you lost this baby? Yes, I know who Liam McGee is, that kid lurking around when Elsa was sitting for his sisters. What do you mean, my arrangement with him? And what do you mean I go east for my company? I just work locally. If Elsa said that, it was just her being upset. She makes things up when she's not at her best. Mr. Stokes, do you remember me? I was good in your class, I got somewhere as you can see. What do you think I would steal a baby for? If the baby is gone somehow, I would do anything I can to help you, but what can I do out here? It's best for Elsa if she gives up on that baby. This book of hers was terrible for her. She wanted it at first, but now she's scared of it. The publisher wants to come see us when he's on the West Coast, but we don't want him to. Elsa wants to forget it. She wants to stay on our beach, keep away from people. I helped her write up those memories for the book. The publisher just took the parts he liked. She wrote lots more. He put that part at the end about us wanting to give the baby a home. She wrote it, but earlier. We didn't mean it to be the last line. Did someone steal the baby because of the book, Mr. Stokes? I'm sorry for you and the mother of the baby. I don't even know what your letter means or how you expect us to do anything about it. Mr. Stokes, it's all been terrible for us too, coming for Anthony's funeral, all of it. Please don't write us anymore, even if you find her. I'm not telling Elsa about your letter. It would be too hard on her. Luckily I opened it before she saw it. I have to protect her.

> Your former student,
> Martin Keeney

"And so no one can know where she is," said Nell by my side reading the letter we'd waited for. When I opened the envelope she had said, "I knew there wouldn't be a picture in it, Burt."

"Nell," I said, stretching my arms to dry the sweat of a hot Saturday morning, "will we go through the rest of our lives never knowing?"

"I think so," she said.

I stared around our sunny living room, the curving inner wall with its marble mantelpiece, the white side walls at their odd angle to each other. I leaned my neck on the back of the couch and followed with my eyes the beautiful curved molding of the outer wall. I stretched my arms back over my head, out to touch the air in the window behind us, Liam's escape. "Can you bear it never knowing?" I asked, dizzy from stretching in the heat.

"I couldn't bear knowing now," she said. "I'm glad I don't have to think of her on that cold beach out there. I'm glad I can't think of her anywhere. Mothers give up their children, Burt. They never know where they are again."

"Fathers even more," I said.

"There are things inside me I don't understand, Burt. There's nothing I really understand. What if there's something in me to hurt even you? Or maybe it's something in me to let you free."

"What?"

"I meet Ladro every day now for lunch during the week."

"Nell—"

"It's a different thing being with him again than with you."

"Nell—" I pulled her close to me in our sweatiness.

"Burt, Burt, Burt—"

"He's your age and you know each other," I said, feeling something beneath my stomach, a kind of surging inside me, tumbling, almost as if it was going to spurt out my mouth. "I've promised you all along—"

"Burt, Burt—" she hummed. She could only say my name, no other words. "Burt—" she said again.

"Nell—"

The word processor should put a big space here.

Our marriage is in the process of being annulled, by agreement, as if I'd never slept with Nell. I feel Ladro has stolen her from me, because his nickname is Italian for thief, as Paula, who now knows everything, pointed out to me in her most recent letter. "But, Burt, it fits in with all your own reservations, doesn't it, really? He's a kindly sort of thief. It's Nell I don't understand. To put that loss behind her, of her own flesh—is it because I'm pregnant I can't imagine it? Because I feel life inside me? Was she too young even to feel it like that, too young to have wanted it so much? Burt? Don't I understand teenagers anymore? God, I'm sure she thinks she and Ladro will have their own now someday, one after another."

Ladro and I spoke quietly on the hilltop, on the library steps, where I'd gone to meet Nell one afternoon. He was hoping to find her there too.

"I haven't seen you since your graduation," I said.

"I saw you," he said, "at the funeral."

"Oh, I saw you too," I said. Why had I forgotten?

"Remember, Mr. Stokes, when I kicked that wastebasket around the john?"

"Why didn't you ever come talk to me after school, Ladro? I kept expecting you'd come talk to me."

"I didn't know what to talk about. I can't talk to you now even."

"About Nell?"

"I never took someone away from someone," he said.

"Is it taking?"

He looked at me but shook his head and looked down.

"What's inside is coming out in front of us," I said. "We can't make it be another way."

"She wants to wait before having another baby," he said. "She wants to work a while and see how it is for us."

I asked him if he'd ever read the Colloquy, which Anthony had given him. He said he'd tried, but he couldn't get past the first page or two. "I keep it by my bed, though," he said.

I asked how things were at the More-For-Less. He'd been made assistant manager, and I told him I'd always known he had it in him. "Nell will tell you I said so years ago," I said.

When Nell came out, with the library's copy of the Obloquy, which she wanted to be the first to borrow, the three of us walked down the hill, and I said I'd treat them to dinner at the Serenata. The waitress wouldn't serve wine to either of them because they weren't twenty. Nell looked like a girl again.

It was an odd dinner, our conversation full of pauses. Nell was still living at the round house, but she'd been to her aunt's a few times, who had said her parents would be willing to see her again, after the annulment. "I won't mind seeing them," Nell said, "if Ladro's there." I thought how glad I was I didn't have to write my parents to explain why I wasn't married anymore. I might go visit them in the fall, I thought. They don't understand why I hadn't been out last year, but I have so little to tell them.

"Will you miss Nell being there?" Ladro asked after a pause, eating the rest of Nell's canoli.

I knew Nell had kept the most private part of our marriage a secret from him, and he thought I had been just her grown-up protector, a kind of selfless person I don't believe really exists. "Of course I will," I said. "I expect I'll see something of both of you, though."

"I told Nell," Ladro said, "if we have a boy, if she doesn't mind, I'd name him Burt after you, for all you did."

"Nell prefers Umberto," I said. "That's a more handsome name than just Burt. Umberto Brown—"

"I'm not thinking about names, Ladro," said Nell.

A couple of months.

And now the last time I'll sit here. This disc has been locked in my desk drawer for too long: Sunday, the first of November, will be the anniversary of Anthony's death. No one knows I won't be here next week. I'll write as late as I want tonight with no one to go home to, and I'll tell the last things that have happened.

A month ago Mrs. Constantinidis left a scribbled note in my mailbox saying she had an offer from the people financing the condominiums in the old schoolhouse. They've already bought the house from the man next door, whom I never spoke to since I first inquired of him who owned the round house. I hadn't noticed he'd moved out. Did he have a wife or live alone?

Mrs. Constantinidis was giving me a month's notice. The contractor already had plans to do the interior work this winter. Interior work? Conversion to one-bedroom apartments, even the basement, and a studio apartment on top. What use will that three-story center hall be to them now? They'll floor it over.

I answered the phone a few weeks ago, late at night in the dark. "Did you get a picture in the mail once?" a voice said far away.

"Liam?"

"Did you?"

"Is she with you?" I asked.

"Not anymore."

"Where are you?"

"Somebody's place. He's out."

"Where?"

"I could say San Antonio," he said.

"Thank you for calling me, Liam." I found myself trembling.

"You told me to call you when I disappeared," he said.

"You won't hang up soon?"

"I can talk on this guy's phone as long as I want. What does he know!"

"If I ask you about that night, you won't hang up?"

"No," he said. His voice was closer now, as if he was holding the receiver right to his lips.

"Where did you go with her?" I asked.

"I can run fast," he said. "I figured you'd head toward my grandmother's building."

"You wouldn't take a baby to your grandmother's—"

"You didn't figure that? Oh, well. See, I met a guy with a car he let me use. I don't have a license. Anyway, then I called him collect from a phone booth and told him where I left his car. What could he do?"

"But the baby must've been freezing!"

"Don't get mad, man."

What a stupid thing for him to say, but I had to listen to him. I was so scared he would hang up.

"She was warm in the car," he said. "I had a basket all ready for her with a blanket from my grandmother's and warm bottles of milk in my grandmother's insulated bag I took. Look, Burt, I went and bought baby bottles and nipples and everything. I bought a box of diapers."

"How far did you go?"

"I planned it out, Burt. I had money I made selling some pictures to that guy at Midnite Books."

"But I didn't give you the pictures."

"You burnt those pictures, you said. Sure you did, man! Well, you can get some better ones when they come out in this book. I got a book too, not just Anthony. Wait'll you see my book! Too bad I'll probably never see it. I got the money though. You go in that bookstore and look. You think I'm lying?"

"What pictures?"

"Some pictures I still had. You'll recognize them. Do you want to hear my story or what?"

I lay back on the pillow. It was too late at night, colder weather coming. I pulled the quilts around me and leaned into the pillow, the receiver on my other ear. "Tell me, Liam," I said.

"I'm real smart," he said. "I had the money, and it was morning then, so I left the car and carried the baby to the place the bus stops, and I just got on."

"With the baby in a basket and bottles!"

"Sure," he said.

"A boy on a bus with a three-week-old baby! Wouldn't they wonder what—"

"Maybe I could look almost like a girl," he said. "Ever think of that, man? I don't go for that sort of thing, but it was my plan, see. You couldn't tell for sure I wasn't a girl, but who's going to check when you got a baby? They just figure you are. They don't want to insult you. I had to leave my jacket in the car, and my boots. Too bad, but I got new better ones now. I had shoes I got from Malinda's closet that fit me sort of tight. I took some blouses and things from her and Isabel when no one was home. I put on some of her lipstick and Malinda's hat and some rings she had and bracelets and Isabel's sunglasses and her long coat. They don't miss things in that mess in their closets—they just wonder where they put them. So I got to Chicago after another night, to some sort of hotel, and then I took my money, being a boy again, and got a room in some place, this little room under the stairs with a smudgy window. I kept the baby there. Guess what I named her? Tony—because I used to want to call Anthony that and he didn't like me to."

"We named her Antonia," I said.

"I just called her Tony."

"And that picture you sent was taken there in that room?"

"It was sort of a bad place, people yelling in the halls. They probably thought I had a wife in there with me too. They didn't care."

"You kept the baby there all the time?"

"When I went out I got this old lady to look after her. I didn't have to explain anything to her, just pay her. She didn't speak English. I sort of pointed and she nods and she goes and sits and rocks Tony in her fat arms. I was getting more money there going out at night. That's a big city."

I thought how I used to go to Chicago when I was young, on a train from the farm, how big the city was, how I thought anything in the world could happen there. "Liam," I said, "but where is she now?"

"I loved having my own baby," he said. "You think I'm not responsible, but I never let that baby in for trouble. She was always happy and warm and had her diapers changed, and I fed her bottles and runny baby food. I played with her all the time. I took her out sometimes with me in the park. People asked if it was my little sister. I said I was baby-sitting my sister's kid. I had interesting talks. I made up all these stories about where I was from, usually Texas, and I was just up here visiting my sister. I pretended I was Tony's father sometimes. I had to explain my wife was really dark and Tony took after her. It got complicated explaining. People heard my accent not being from Chicago and not Texas, but I told them how much I moved as a kid. I loved when I got someone thinking I was her father. And listen, I never brought anybody back to the room. She didn't see anything like that happening, just that old lady baby-sitting and me playing with her all the time. I borrowed some guy's camera and took those pictures I sent you one of. That shows you what a happy kid she was. You can see what a good father I was."

"But where is she, Liam?"

"I miss her too," he said. "I didn't want to give her up, but it was getting colder up there again. I didn't see staying there, and I didn't want to go through looking like a girl again. And what am I going to do when she gets older and starts to crawl? She was getting five months old or something. I was reading up in some book I got about babies. I'd be reading it and getting all worried looking ahead chapters. I'd sit there and hold her in this little room we had under the stairs and talk to her in baby language I made up for her. She looked like Anthony, all dark, looking at me. See, Burt, you think I don't care about anything, but I cared about keeping Tony myself and always having her. You wonder how'd I explain to her someday who she was? I had it figured out. I'd tell her she's my little sister and our parents died in a fire when she was just born, and if she remembered that old lady I'd say that was our grandmother who took care of us, then she died too, but she was the only relative we had, so then we were on our own, and I brought her up myself. By then I'd be having a

regular job, and she'd go to school. I made up a new name for
our family. Cook I said it was, when I had to take her once to a
clinic because she was crying all the time with some cold. I saw a
sign with Cook County on it, so that was the name I told them. I
was her father, I said, and her mother was sick, too, at home, and
I was unemployed, so we weren't on a medical plan. They
thought I was weird, but what could they do? They see all
kinds."

"You thought I'd have the police out looking for a kid named
McGee?"

"You, or somebody. I might be on some list."

"Where is she, Liam?"

"You keep wanting me to tell you."

"Of course I do." He was making me so scared, not telling me.

"You don't tell me anything," he said. "I don't know how it
happened after you ran out in your underpants. I just saw you,
and I got around the corner. I'm not going to tell you till you tell
me something. I'm not going to hang up. That guy's out, I told
you."

"We didn't go to the police," I said.

"I figured you went to my grandmother and got her all crazy
but then if you went to the police, well, I figured you'd go, but
after a while, like in the morning. You'd be sure first it wasn't
like I wanted money or I'd expose you for perverting innocent
kids. Because if I just wanted something from you, you'd give it.
That's what you probably thought. You never thought I just
wanted the baby for myself and that was all."

"This is what we thought, Liam: We thought Elsa had you
take the baby. We had a letter from her about how she should
have Anthony's child with her, how Martin was coming east for
his company and he'd get our baby."

"Well, you know what that Martin Keeney is. He couldn't get
his head out between her legs long enough."

"We thought somehow he found you and you said you'd do it
for them, or maybe you wrote them, or called them, out there,
and you gave them the idea after you'd been to see me, or—"

"You got a letter from Elsa, and you thought it was her and
Martin!"

"We thought they had you do it, or you did it for them, for money."

"That's dumb," Liam said. "So why didn't you go to the police?"

"Nell said no."

"I thought it was you said no."

"I think Nell was out of her mind then," I said. "She couldn't do anything. She waved her hands in the air and stared and trembled all over, for weeks. Liam, if you could've seen what you did to her—"

"Don't tell me what I did to her, man," he said.

"Where's Antonia, Liam!" I said, loud into the receiver.

"You think you're the only one who loved Anthony, you and that Nell. But who loved Anthony before anyone else? You don't even know what it was like when we were kids. We grew up together. We played every day since I was five. Till I was fifteen, man—that's longer than you knew him, you or Nell. You know how long it feels like when you're a kid? When you're fifteen you think five is eighty years ago, you think it's all your life. So you knew him a couple years, Burt, so Nell knew him in high school a couple years—I knew him always, Burt, always, every day, almost like brothers. You don't think I miss him more than you? You think about that one, man! Everything I remember when I was a kid, every year with Anthony, meeting after school, walking home, playing, riding our bikes, getting in trouble, laughing at his duck talk, sitting at Mass side by side, wrestling, hanging around on Saturdays— Don't give me him being such a big part in your life!"

"He grew away from you, Liam—"

"See, and I lost him even before you ever lost anything, him or his baby. See how long I been missing him!"

"Why take his baby, Liam?"

"And you didn't go to the police," Liam said. "What did you ever do? You didn't save her baby for her. You didn't do anything for me, did you? You didn't save me. You don't think you could've saved me? You could've. What do you think I was doing when I ran down from your roof crying and you came to me and

I pulled your hands around and started kissing them? What do you think I was doing? What do you think?"

I didn't know what to say to him. I was trembling and tingling down my arms.

"You thought I was just lying there waiting for you, Burt, right, to let you do what you wanted."

"Everything we did, Liam, you wanted too," I said. "You always showed me what you wanted, more than I ever knew."

"I showed you!"

"You showed me how—"

"No!" he shouted, making the receiver fuzz in my ear.

"Liam—"

"You didn't say you loved me."

"You didn't say you loved me," I said.

"I wouldn't dare to say it," he said. "How could I be the one to say it?"

"How could I be?" I said. "You went out every night doing I don't know what. What would you do with me? You were a kid—"

"So what if I went out! That's nothing to do with it. I worked on your house a whole year, all the time with you. That's where I lived. Where else did I live? And you lose your job for that Nell, who's some dumb kid you teach and she's going out with your great Anthony. And you probably never been with girls before—"

"What if I wanted a child, too?" I said.

"What if I wanted a child!" he yelled back to me.

"Liam—"

"I can just hang up."

"Where is she, Liam? Please tell me."

"So you can tell Nell and come get her?"

"Nell doesn't live with me anymore. We're having our marriage annulled," I said.

"You want an award?"

I turned on my other side, my whole body feeling achy. I leaned on the receiver into the pillow.

"Tony had a good home," he said. "You think I didn't cry for days figuring what to do? You think I didn't sit in that room holding Tony and crying over her?"

"I don't think that, Liam."

"There's people that pay for a baby," he said. "There's people that want to have their own baby and can't have one and they'll do anything, even illegal. I met all kinds of guys in Chicago. They knew these things. This one guy paid me if I got him a baby and he'd get all the fake papers and somehow he'd get her to a good home, he said, where they had money for a beautiful girl like Tony."

I started crying down into the phone. I couldn't control it.

"You think I didn't cry too, Burt, all the time for days? And I thought and I thought, and I knew I couldn't do it any other way—"

Gulping, I said, "You could send her back to me—"

"Not to you, Burt," he said. "I couldn't send her to you. I can't ever send you anything. You know why I let this man here beat me?"

"What, Liam, what—"

"This place I'm staying—"

"San Antonio?"

"I just said that, San Antonio, because of Anthony. I could be anywhere."

"Where are you, Liam? Why do you let him beat you?"

"Why I let him beat me? I let him. I want him to. Because of you, Burt. Because of Anthony. Because of you."

"Liam, I thought you wanted everything we did. I didn't want you doing anything you didn't want. What did you want?" I couldn't stop my crying. I kept crying into the receiver and tried to say things: "If I could've seen you with that baby—you were happy with her then? If I could see you—"

I didn't hear if he had hung up, but it was quiet on the line. My other ear was muffled in the pillow. I waited in quietness as my crying stopped. Slowly I moved the receiver from my ear, leaned up on one elbow into the window's dim light, placed the receiver on the phone, picked it up again, listened to it buzz, put it back again. I rolled myself into one of the quilts as I swung my cold legs off the bed. I stood on the bare floor.

I took some steps, toward the window, then toward the door to the hall. First, I leaned over the bannister in darkness, then I put

my hand on the rail and climbed slowly to the third floor. I stood
at the top, leaned over again, could see nothing. Above there was
a dimly lit night sky through the skylight. The quilt was like my
robe, hanging to my ankles. I felt over to where the stepladder
was and pulled it to the landing, tested its braces, began to climb
shakily in the dark. I stood on the next-to-top step and reached
up, touching the Plexiglas, which was crackling between the
rising warmth of the round house and the cold night air. Balancing,
I listened to it, the faintest crackles it made. I stayed there for
minutes.

Then I stepped down two steps and leaned myself forward,
over the top step, and felt for the round rungs on the other side of
the ladder, where Liam had hung by his elbows. Blood came to
my forehead, upside down. I stayed for minutes that way, too,
then slipped dizzily back up and over and down the ladder to
stand on the floor. I felt for the stairs with my toes.

I thought of the empty house I was coming down into, and I
was scared now to be alone there at night. I touched the switch
on the second-floor landing and saw I had taken the brown quilt,
not the blue one, saw the empty center hall, stairs curving up,
stairs curving down. I flipped the switch back to darkness.

I felt along the curved wall, past the bathroom, past Nell's
room and Antonia's room, doors closed, and down the stairs
again, taking slow steps, the fridge humming in the kitchen. I
passed back under the stairs, along the wall of the hall, a street
lamp out the dining-room window, darkness in the windows in
the living room with curtains drawn, around past the front door,
to the door beside the kitchen that led down again.

In my humming basement, in complete darkness, I felt with
my toes on the smudgy floor. I reached about for the furnace
switch and flipped it off, then for the fuse box and cut off
everything. In the quiet I began to see one square not quite as
dark as the darkness I was in, a basement window with a plastic
sheet stapled over it for insulation. I felt my way to it, touched it,
smooth, cold. I stood there for minutes more.

I thought how I could go up and down the stairs, to the top, to
the bottom, to the top, to the bottom, holding the quilt to me, all
night long. I was tired. I still heard Liam's voice, but no words. I

sat, and later I fell asleep leaning against the wall. I went back up to bed in the early morning.

Paula writes me, in my renewed bachelorhood, and she says that I have finally stripped it down to the bare surface of all things in my life. "You're back to your monkishness again but knowing more what love should have been, Burt. Not the love you gave Anthony, with all it did for him, or the careful love for Nell. And then that love, whatever it was, for Liam, well—" But I think how Liam's alone somewhere as I read her letter. I look back down at it: "Why don't you start in a new place, Burt, Providence even? Or what about that woman at work, Faye, who seems to like you so? But stay with adults now—as much as anyone is ever entirely adult, Frank would say. What is it you've been looking for, Burt? The selfishness of your youth? Something that didn't happen then? The parts that didn't come together?"

Paula has decided I am Umbertocchini. She and Frank are hardly the Count and Countess, that was just Anthony's whimsy, his tribute to the Innocenzi, she says, but that music master— I don't think so, I write her back. Yes, Anthony did tell me he wanted to write about me one day, but I'm sure that the last manifestation of an Umberto, that Umbertocchini, is once again his father, a kindlier manifestation this time, perhaps, perhaps the father he'd wished for, but not me.

After a few days of calling in sick, of lying in bed after Liam's call, the TV on, but not watching it, I remembered through all his words something he'd said about selling some photographs. I went downtown, had two beers first at the Brew 'n' Burger, then went into the Spondee, or Midnite Books, whichever name it goes by now. I didn't know where to look. There was plenty of what I'd expected, but all sealed in plastic so you couldn't leaf through. The part of the store that was the old Spondee still sold what they called literature, including a few copies each of Anthony's first two books and stacks of the Letters, marked down, but not the Trochee's Obloquy. I saw a shelf labeled Erotica and glanced along it. There was even a book by Sarah Bowen called Memoirs Of A Cleaning Lady. I pulled out a book of photographs called From Every Angle, Kitchell's latest.

The photographs were of parts of bodies, a rougher bigger

body, hair on its legs and chest, and what I thought was a girl's soft body, but then I turned the next page and I was looking down the flatness of my own bare chest to the crouching thighs of Liam, lowering himself onto me. It was the set of pictures I took that Liam said hadn't come out. He had shown me blank negatives, but that must have been one of his deceptions. I bought the book, keeping an eye out in case Kitchell came out of the back room, thinking he probably wouldn't recognize Burt Something anyway.

And no one would recognize me from those pictures. The curved walls of the round house don't even show because the bodies are so close up, so entangled. Only the different tones of our skins let you tell who is who. There's an anonymous love poem, a line or so a page, but I haven't bothered reading it through. Liam's face is at odd angles to the camera, flung back, bent down with his hair spreading over his eyes. Or I see my own glance down our sides to tangled legs. The stepladder is in one picture, but only a rung, his elbows hooked around it, his shoulders and skinny chest straining as he hangs there, his chin and nostrils seen from below, my fingers— I look at these pictures every night.

Now I'll finish my work, take home the last photo of Antonia and my copy of the Letters and leave this disc in its slipcase on Faye's desk. Monday morning she'll find it with the title I'll write on it, to let her know where I've gone, but not so she can find me, not so anyone can find me.

Paula and Francesco, parents-to-be, are coming to visit tomorrow, bringing advance copies of the Obsequy for me, and Frank has made paper-bag masks for the three of us when we answer the door tomorrow evening to trick-or-treaters. Then Sunday, they are to help me move to the new apartment I told them I've rented. Paula is too pregnant to carry heavy things, but she'll do more than she should, Frank says. They both took my long letter of explanation—about the baby, about Nell and Ladro, about Liam—with such understanding and love for me, I don't feel I deserve them.

Their bus will get in at five. By the time they take the city bus from downtown, transfer to the bus along the avenue and walk up to the round house, it will be near six. What will they find?

I saw Mrs. Constantinidis on the street last week, struggling along with her groceries. "I got your note," I said.

"It's legal," she said, setting the bags down on either side of her, leaning them up against her legs.

"I know it is, Mrs. Constantinidis."

"I need money for my old dad, his hospital bills—"

"Don't make an excuse, Mrs. Constantinidis. I'm moving."

"I saw your wife moved out, some time back," she said with a slight smile.

"She's already in the new place."

"Is she, Mr. Stokes? How they do come and go!"

"I'll be gone by the first," I said.

Mrs. Constantinidis once threatened to burn the house down for the insurance. The contractor is going to ruin it anyway, moldings stripped off, recessed indirect lighting, huge plate-glass windows for the views—I'd burn it first, pour turpentine all down the staircase, fill the air with cooking gas—an inferno. Could I be that furious?

And when I've stopped my writing here, will I start to feel guilty? My biggest question—as long as the writing is true, I'm forgiven, says Anthony. But I can't write what comes last before I have done it, so I can only guess the next truth. I will have to break into—my imagination?

This only:

I went home, and I spent all the late night with the pictures of Liam in my arms. What didn't I do for him? I thought. Where can I find him? Will I go to San Antonio for a start and look for traces of him? Chicago? Liam Cook— Is it possible to find someone hiding in this huge country?

Will I burn the house and make them think I wanted to die by fire? But no traces of me in the ashes— Might I do such a thing and have the police looking for me everywhere I went? How shall I not be there when Paula and Frank arrive? Paula has been telling me to go somewhere else for a long while. She will reassure Nell and Ladro, tell them it was what I needed. And they will all expect to be hearing from me soon.

No one will know I have gone to find Liam until Faye prints out this disc, and then I will be as lost to them all as Liam is lost to me. What name will I take? Or I could kill myself, leap in front of a bus. I could even burn myself down with my house, if I wanted to.

The only thing I know to put on this screen is that I went home, and I spent all night until sunrise on my bed and stared at Liam's body, however entangled, alone before me—aching, submissive.